'Things aren't always as straightforward as they seem.'

'True. I suppose you're going to say that sexual attraction is a strange, uncontrollable urge, and that you simply couldn't help yourself?'

'No! It was nothing like that! It was nothing to do with sex!' Henrietta's outburst turned a few curious heads their way, and Nick's arms tightened slightly around her. His gaze was penetrating as he looked down at her agitated face.

'You don't like dancing with me?'

'To be honest, I consider it beyond the call of duty. I'd rather be talking to Marc. At least he appears to know elementary good manners.'

'And he'd also like to add you to his long list of extramarital affairs. This could be his lucky night—he's found himself a lady with plenty of experience in such matters!'

Lashing out with her hand wasn't a premeditated thing, it just came as a furious reaction to the goading words. Her palm connected with stinging accuracy, and her fingers tingled as she dropped her arm and stared at the darkening patch on Nick's cheek.

PRIVATE PROPERTY

BY
ROSALIE ASH

MILLS & BOON LIMITED
ETON HOUSE   18-24 PARADISE ROAD
RICHMOND   SURREY   TW9 1SR

*First published in Great Britain 1991
by Mills & Boon Limited*

© Rosalie Ash 1991

*Australian copyright 1991
Philippine copyright 1991
This edition 1991*

ISBN 0 263 77038 9

*Set in Times Roman 10 on 12 pt.
01-9103-53942 C*

Made and printed in Great Britain

CHAPTER ONE

IT WAS going to be strange, seeing Nick Trevelyan again. Henrietta's pre-interview nerves wavered into genuine apprehension for a moment, before they were firmly controlled. Calm down, she warned herself silently, reaching up to smooth the French pleat confining her heavy, streaky blonde hair, and surreptitiously wiping damp palms on the skirt of her khaki suit. Stay composed, stay in control.

She was being ridiculous. She was letting the past rule her life. If she was going to anticipate hostility and disapproval everywhere she went, she'd be better off cutting her losses and going away. And in spite of everything, she didn't want to go away again. She loved Cornwall. She had as many friends as critics, and her family home was here—the cheerful, chaotic vicarage with its constant stream of visitors and her parents and her brother and sisters, admittedly sometimes irritating and overpowering, but still her family, and no amount of local gossip and malicious rumour would drive her away. It had become a point of honour, over the last four years. And an interview with someone vaguely connected with Tristan's family, a remote face from the past whom she'd only met two or three times in her entire life, certainly wasn't going to deter her from the chance of a top-paid job which fitted her qualifications and ambitions to the letter.

'You can go in now, Mrs Melyn.'

'Thank you.'

As the girl spoke, she swung the inner office door ajar, and Henrietta could see a gleaming wood-block floor and a wide expanse of antique Wilton carpet waiting to be crossed before any sign of the office's occupant came into view.

The office was enormous, high-ceilinged and Victorian, and full of antique furniture, but Henrietta didn't notice any details, apart from the man seated silently at an enormous mahogany desk. The warm May sun was slanting in through a window behind him, making it difficult to see his face. But his gaze appeared to be coolly upon her as she went across the room towards him, and she felt absurdly conscious of her own body, of the provocative swing of her hips as she tried to move smoothly and elegantly in the new tan court shoes she'd bought specially for the occasion.

Arriving in front of the desk, she hesitated, staring at the hard, calculating expression on the dark face with a jolt of dismay, and a rapidly sinking heart. So Nick Trevelyan *did* listen to gossip, she reflected bleakly. So much for the blithe assumption that she was becoming paranoid about people's opinions of her in this closed, parochial part of the North Cornish coast.

'Sit down, Mrs Melyn.' The deep voice was cool as dark brown silk. She sat down carefully on the over-stuffed leather chair, and cleared her throat nervously.

'Thank you.' That sounded inane, and she bit her lip ruefully. Was that all she could find to say? The daunting silence pressed in on her, and her polite smile met with no response. Annoyance began to overcome nerves. Of all things, she disliked people who adopted the technique of stony silence to force others into indiscreet babble. Drawing a steadying breath, she decided to take the lead, since Nick Trevelyan seemed determined to make her sweat it out.

'I've come about the post of bilingual secretary. But you know that, of course! Do you have my references and curriculum vitae in front of you? I've brought a spare copy in case they were mislaid.'

She began to open her neat tan leather clutch-bag, and he lifted a lean brown hand in an impatient motion.

'That won't be necessary, Mrs Melyn. I have your details in front of me.'

'Then . . . is there something wrong, Mr Trevelyan?'

'Not at all, Mrs Melyn.'

She glanced at him swiftly, challengingly, catching the sardonic note in his voice. Meeting his long-lidded ice-green eyes was a slight shock to her system, and with a stab of surprise she found herself remembering their occasional meetings, over the years, and wondering if he remembered them as well.

Their eyes seemed to have locked for an endless moment, and he must have read her mind, because he said suddenly, 'I was just thinking how time changes people.' The cold flash of a smile came nowhere near to making his eyes smile too. 'I knew you years ago, when you were a little kid with a pigtail. You were always chasing your dog on to Trevelyan land. I hoisted him out of a deserted mill-sluice once. But I'm sure you don't remember that.' The reminiscence lacked any normal warmth or amusement.

She laughed slightly, determined to retain her composure. Was he deliberately trying to disconcert her?

'As a matter of fact, I do remember. My Labrador Sammy got stuck in Trebethick Mill, and you rode up on a big horse, like the Lone Ranger to the rescue!'

He'd suggested they take off their belts to tie round Sammy, and she'd been wearing her big brother's jeans, which promptly slid down to her ankles. She forebore from reminding him of that detail, but how could she forget the experience?

'How old would you have been?' The green eyes were narrowed assessingly. 'Twelve?'

'Good heavens, I really can't remember!' she lied brightly, not prepared to admit that the whole episode had just come back to mind in graphic detail. Her birthday was in August, and she'd been just fourteen, that summer, and Nick Trevelyan had been a devastatingly attractive man of around twenty, on a rare visit home from his London college to see his family. His suppressed amusement at her plight had stayed strangely imprinted on her brain, now she came to think about it.

'All I remember is that I found the episode quite mortifying!' She spoke lightly, resisting the temptation to digress further down memory lane with this cool stranger facing her across the desk. Had she ever called him *Nick*? He could only be seven years older than she was, but the thought of being on such casual first-name terms with this man now was unthinkable.

'Mortifying?' One dark eyebrow slanted as he gazed at her implacably.

'Well, yes! Teenage girls don't relish losing their trousers in front of young men!' The laughing words were out before she could stop them, and Henrietta swallowed abruptly, the mocking coolness in Nick Trevelyan's face reminding her sharply that she was supposed to be participating in a formal interview. But he'd started it, she reassured herself silently. She could hardly be penalised for chipping in with her side of the story!

Nick Trevelyan's wide mouth twitched slightly at the corners, but it was hard to say whether he was amused or annoyed. She fidgeted slightly on her seat, watching the long-fingered brown hand toying idly with a heavy brass paperknife on the leather-topped desk. Suddenly a host of other memories resurrected themselves, things she'd put to the back of her mind and forgotten in the rigorous demands of adult life. Some time after the Sammy episode, the following year, she'd gone to the Christmas party at the Melyns', as Tristan Melyn's guest, and Nick Trevelyan had been there, with a sultry red-haired woman. He'd been recovering from the car accident when he'd been badly injured, and his older brother Bevan had been killed... and she remembered Tristan remarking on how different Nick looked. It hadn't just been to do with the scars on his face and hand. They'd privately agreed he'd aged at least five years...

'According to your references...' Nick's dark head bent to peruse the papers before him '...you've had four jobs so far. And you only left secretarial college two and a half years ago. Isn't that rather a lot of chopping and changing, Mrs Melyn?'

Henrietta tensed slightly. 'Possibly. But they've all been upward progressions. To get promotion you need to keep moving around.'

'So you're ambitious? Do you see yourself jumping from secretarial to managerial level if the opportunity arises?'

It was an innocent enough question. But Nick Trevelyan seemed to weigh it down with sarcastic mockery, so that it felt like a taunting accusation.

'Who knows?' She shrugged slightly. 'I certainly wouldn't turn down any offers.'

Nick Trevelyan stood up, slowly straightening to an intimidating height. The sun fell on the left side of his face, highlighting the silvery lines of the small scars on his temple and upper lip, and her eyes went instinctively to his left hand, where the disfigurement still showed across the tendons of his fingers, jolting her memory yet again. He walked around to lean casually against the edge of the desk, close to her. The odd wave of body-awareness returned without warning. Henrietta found she was imperceptibly drawing herself inwards, compressing her ankles and knees and clasping her hands primly in her lap, and at the same time wondering what on earth was the matter with her. Staring up at him, her face composed into its normal good-humoured smile, she briefly searched around for an explanation of his strange effect on her. Why should this man, with his bitter cynicism, his brooding air of condemnation, touch some special sort of chord inside her?

He'd noticed her staring at his hand, and he pushed both hands into the pockets of his immaculately cut grey suit trousers, so that her attention was reluctantly caught instead by the taut stretch of the fine wool cloth over powerful thighs.

'So you're open to any offers, Mrs Melyn?' The contempt was unmistakable. She felt heat seep into her cheeks, and lifted her chin defensively.

'I'm available for the job as advertised, Mr Trevelyan. If promotion came my way, I'd have to weigh up the pros and cons.'

'I'm not offering a stepping-stone to greater things, Mrs Melyn. I want a personal secretary who is totally reliable, totally loyal, experienced and capable, and able to work under pressure. I also require someone fluent in French and Spanish. An ability to spell would also be desirable.' The cold green gaze raked her face impassively.

Her cheeks were growing hotter, but she smiled at him politely.

'I left Graystone Abbey with A Levels in French, Spanish and economics. My grandmother was French, so I've spent a lot of time in France, and I'm fluent in that language. My Spanish is fairly good . . . and you can judge my secretarial skills from my application form.'

'I'm sure I can. But refresh my memory.'

'RSA Grade Three typing, one hundred and twenty w.p.m. shorthand. I'm well-versed in all modern office technology, and I hold a Private Secretary's Diploma.'

'And why do you want to work for Trevelyan Estates?'

'I'm not sure I do yet, Mr Trevelyan,' she murmured calmly, mentally crossing her fingers that standing up to his brow-beating approach might be the kind of reaction he was looking for. 'But my last two jobs were with estate agencies, and I enjoy working for auctioneers and estate agents. The work tends to be varied and interesting. Your firm is the largest surviving independent agent in Cornwall. And the appointment agency stressed your involvement with Europe, which I find challenging . . .'

'With A Levels like yours I'm surprised you didn't go on to study languages at university, Mrs Melyn.'

'I . . . I had planned to . . .' Did he already know all this, but was just putting her through it? Nick Trevelyan clearly had a wide streak of sadism running through his personality.

'So why didn't you?'

'I got married instead.' She lifted a calm, candid face to meet his scathing appraisal. 'Maybe I'm developing a persecution complex, but I feel sure you must already know this. Everyone else in North Cornwall seems to know it, and the Melyns are hardly unknown in the county! I married Tristan Melyn shortly after I left school.'

'Ah, yes. It was a whirlwind romance, wasn't it? I do seem to recall some talk circulating the county gatherings.'

'Yes. A lot of people said we were rather young to rush into marriage,' she agreed tonelessly. 'But I'm not sure this has anything to do with my being suitable for the job you're offering, Mr Trevelyan.'

'On the contrary, Mrs Melyn. I like to reassure myself that my staff possess the necessary strength of character to perform their job efficiently.' The words were purred, rather than spoken. She stiffened, struggling with the desire to stand up and express polite disinterest in the job on offer. Until now, Nick Trevelyan had been a hazy name from the past, a face she vaguely recalled from her impressionable teenage years. Now she realised she could never have even remotely known him. She certainly hadn't appreciated how ruthlessly unpleasant he could be, in spite of Piers's joking words of caution the other night.

'So... you married at eighteen, and you were a widow at nineteen, if local gossip serves me well?'

'Yes...' She got abruptly to her feet, and found herself standing far too close to Nick Trevelyan's lounging form. Her hip brushed accidentally against the hard bulge of his thigh muscle, and she stepped back as if she'd been burnt. 'That's right. Tristan and I were married for precisely eleven months. Then he had one too many drinks at a party, staggered home along the Thames embankment, and fell in and drowned, leaving the tabloid Press to amass all the gossip about our marriage and decide his life with me must have been so ghastly that death was the only possible option! I do apologise for not including all this vital information on my curriculum vitae, Mr Trevelyan. I mistakenly assumed it was just my qualifications and *secretarial* experience I needed to itemise!'

She turned to leave, appalled at the warning prickle of tears at the back of her eyes, the growing lump in her throat, but Nick Trevelyan's hand reached out to take hold of her arm, and she froze.

'There's no need to get over-emotional, Mrs Melyn. But if we're going to work together, these things are best out in the open.'

'Really? So you're about to give me a full account of your own personal and domestic arrangements, are you, Mr Trevelyan?'

Something flashed in the cold green eyes, and he dropped his hand abruptly from her arm. She moved away carefully, controlling her breathing with difficulty. How had a simple interview turned into this dangerous confrontation between two virtual strangers? She could hardly believe it was happening.

'I am considering employing you, Mrs Melyn. Not the other way around.'

'Oh, yes. Of course. How naïve of me to get muddled up!'

' "Naïve" is not an adjective I'd use in your case. You appear quite worldly wise to me. And you must surely be used to people asking you about your marriage. Please sit down again, Mrs Melyn.'

His calm air of control in such an emotionally charged atmosphere left her speechless, and she did as she was told. Surreptitiously she extracted a tissue from her clutch-bag, and blew her nose, and Nick Trevelyan appeared to have sufficient consideration to allow her a few minutes to compose herself.

'Let me tell you a little more about the job,' he said curtly, when she next met his eyes. 'I need a secretary who has no domestic ties, who can travel at a moment's notice, work anti-social hours, staying late in the evenings sometimes, some weekend work. On business trips to France I require an alert pair of extra ears. My French is moderately fluent, but there are occasions when I need verification. I'm engaged in some delicate negotiations and I wouldn't want to make a bloody fool of myself through a language misunderstanding. Do you think you're up to that?'

'There shouldn't be any problem.'

'Another point. The fact that your brother Piers has worked for me for the past six years could lead to a conflict of loyalties. I would expect total discretion regarding business and personal matters, Mrs Melyn.'

The scathing tone made her jerk her head up again, her gold-brown eyes flashing sparks of anger. 'The diploma I hold from the London Chamber of Commerce should reassure you on that score, Mr Trevelyan. I am a fully qualified *private* secretary!'

'Fine. In return for all that, I'm offering an above-average salary——' he named a figure which made her head reel '—and six weeks' annual holiday, plus statutory bank holidays. How much notice would you have to give, if I offered you the job?'

'I'd have to give a month's notice, naturally. If I was offered the job, and if I decided to accept it.' Pride was something she could ill afford, she reflected wryly, but the words were out before she could restrain herself.

'I need someone to start in a fortnight's time, Mrs Melyn.'

'That's hardly realistic, Mr Trevelyan. No one worth employing would be prepared to leave their present employer in the lurch like that.'

Her voice was cool, and she met his eyes levelly, seeing the flicker of mocking awareness there. He knew she was being deliberately difficult, her aloofness bordering on insolence. Was she totally mad? Henrietta breathed in deeply, and weighed up the astronomic salary, generous holidays, and exciting prospect of the work involved, against the awesome prospect of having Nicholas Trevelyan as her boss. Money wasn't everything, but the salary he was offering would certainly transform her standard of living from breadline to moderately well-off.

'I have a couple of other interviews lined up, in any case,' she heard herself adding, almost defensively.

'I see. Have I deeply offended you, Mrs Melyn?' His voice was suddenly rougher, with a note of grudging amusement. 'Do I detect a polite brush-off?'

'Not at all. If you offer me the job, naturally I'll consider it seriously.'

'Good.' He sauntered round the desk again, and walked across to the window. She watched him, reluctantly drawn by the lithe control in his movements. 'Have you brought a shorthand notebook?'

He had his back to her, revealing a daunting width of shoulder beneath the smoothly expensive cut of his suit jacket.

'Yes . . .' With shaking fingers she delved quickly into her bag and produced book and pencil, waiting with thumping heart for the gruelling test she knew would come. Sure enough, Nick Trevelyan dictated at machine-gun speed a short letter in English querying outstanding commission fees with a vendor, another complicated business letter in fluent French, and a third in rapid, confident but slightly erratic Spanish. With curt instructions to transcribe her shorthand, and translate the English letter into both foreign languages, she found herself dismissed.

She hastily grabbed her bag and got up.

'See my present secretary, Gillian, about the practical test. I've got your telephone number on your application form. I'll be in touch.'

'Thank you...' She paused at the door, a sudden thought striking her. 'Can I ask why your present secretary, Gillian, is leaving, Mr Trevelyan?' A nervous breakdown? Chronic depression? She didn't quite dare to make the sarcastic suggestions, but her brown eyes were cool as she waited for his explanation.

'Gillian is getting married. She'll be looking for a less demanding job.'

'Oh, I see...' The breathtaking chauvinism of him! Naturally he couldn't be expected to employ a secretary likely to divide her time between a husband and her boss! 'Well, goodbye, Mr Trevelyan.'

And you can go to hell, she added silently, marching past him out of the door and feeling an enormous wave of exhaustion wash over her, as if she'd spent the last twenty minutes wrestling with a tiger.

Three hours later, surrounded by the irrepressible hubbub of a family party in the idyllic setting of her parents' garden, she felt only marginally more relaxed. Somehow Nick Trevelyan's coiled-up tension had infected her. She felt abnormally jumpy and irritable.

Ashamed of herself, she resisted all the usual entreaties to sit down and relax, instead flinging herself whole-heartedly into sandwich-cutting, tea-making, games-organising, and assiduously clearing away used plates and glasses, preferring to leave the socialising side to the rest of the Beauman clan.

It was the twins' tenth birthday, and among other things they'd received brand-new tennis rackets, and were enthusiastically, if not very accurately, conducting a game of tennis on the grass court beyond the orchard. Their shrieks of merriment were being matched only by the high volume of quick-fire conversation and accompanying laughter being exchanged between the adult members of the family, and their respective partners, who were sitting in a sprawling circle in the warm evening sun.

The golden family, people called them. Varying shades of blond, all of them, with no trace anywhere of the distant strain of French blood through Henrietta's mother's side. Her sister Helen, ten years her senior, with her honey-coloured waves neatly caught back from her head with tortoiseshell combs, was deep in earnest conversation with her husband. Her brother Piers, straight fair hair flopping over sleepy blue eyes, was lounging on a garden chair with his usual lazy panache, his latest girlfriend Josie adoringly feeding him cucumber sandwiches. The twins, with their white-blonde plaits, were careering around the tennis court in the distance. Henrietta decided her own brindled mane, with its natural streaks of dark and light, was the only clue to the blend of nationalities.

Having handed round the drinks and food, she was starting to load empty dishes on to the tray to return to the kitchen when Helen leapt to her feet in exasperation.

'Hetti, will you stop waiting on everyone and come and sit down?' Firmly removing the tray from her hands, she steered her to a chair. 'Come and enjoy the sunshine. We can clear this lot away later. You're making me feel terribly guilty!'

'She always makes me feel guilty!' drawled Piers, lighting a Gauloise and closing his eyes. 'She's such a little beaver, aren't you, Hett?'

'Well, if I'm a beaver, that must make you a dormouse.'

'Mmm. Family gatherings here always remind me of the Mad Hatter's Tea Party. Mother's the Queen, Father's the Mad Hatter, Helen's the Duchess, I'm the Dormouse, and darling little Hetti can be Alice.'

'Thank you, Piers. But I don't think all those characters actually *appeared* in the Mad Hatter's Tea Party!'

'Go back to sleep, Piers!' Helen advised. 'Or preferably go away and reread the twins' copy of *Alice in Wonderland*! I want to talk to Henrietta about her interview today. How did it go?'

Piers sat up a little straighter, with an air of having forgotten something very important.

'Ah, yes, I meant to ask—how did it go, Hetti? How did you get on with the fearsome Trevelyan?'

'I didn't get on with him at all. In fact I think he's put me off interviews for life!' Henrietta exchanged a rueful glance with Helen, suddenly aware that her mother was glancing over, a worried expression clouding her warm brown eyes.

'Well, I did warn you!' Piers crowed. 'Did he realise who you were? Did he twig you were my little sister, I mean?'

'Of course he knew who I was. We'd met once or twice in the dim and distant past. And I'm hardly your *little* sister now, Piers! You're only three years older than I am, and I'm twenty-three!'

'You're very touchy tonight, Hett. After all, until the surprise package twins arrived late on the scene, you were the baby of the family!' teased Piers, adding thoughtfully, 'So...things didn't go too well, then?'

'You could say that.'

'He's not that bad once you're in with him,' Piers drawled loftily. 'Speaking as one of his up and coming branch managers, tipped most likely to succeed, with the juicy prospect of a junior partnership looming ahead, I think I can vouch for Trevelyan's finer points!'

Henrietta felt goaded. 'Branch manager to partner in one leap strikes me as rather an ambitious idea.'

'Well, I'm an ambitious guy,' Piers grinned, 'I've got a lifestyle to maintain—I need plenty of lovely money to fund it!'

How much of this was for Josie's rapt benefit? Henrietta wondered, as her mother murmured predictably,

'Money isn't everything, Piers, dear!'

Piers looked unrepentant. 'But Nick's a fantastic guy to work for, once you've won his respect. Think positive, Hetti, love, and you could be rich, like me!'

Henrietta gazed at her brother with a touch of impatience. Piers might be her senior, but he still seemed rather immature. He tended to make contentious remarks on purpose, to trigger the inevitable parental lectures. Four years ago she would probably have sided with Piers, purely to establish her right to think as she pleased, but she'd learned her lesson the hard way when she ran off and married Tristan...now she found herself agreeing with her mother, for all the world as if she were the elder of the two—Piers seemed far too wrapped up in his expensive cars and lavish lifestyle, and it was slightly worrying.

'Well, all I can say is, it was the worst interview I've ever endured!' she retorted coolly. 'Nick Trevelyan's a...a bully! An absolute pig!'

There was a brief silence, and she realised with a sinking heart that she'd allowed her tension to filter through, because she could almost hear the family mentally closing ranks around her, fiercely loyal and protective of her. Helen's doctor husband Hugo was suddenly eyeing her with his 'professional counselling' expression, and her father had lowered the theological paper he was studying, and flipped off his gold-rimmed glasses to peer at her in concern. Henrietta wanted to run and hide. They all loved her so much, and since Tristan died they were all so keen to help, but it somehow made her feel worse. She didn't *deserve* this! After all the trouble she'd caused her family in the past, there was no way she deserved this unconditional loyalty and protectiveness...

'Never mind, darling,' her mother said quietly, 'don't let one bad experience deter you. Plenty more good jobs around! And if you stayed where you are, you wouldn't be doing so badly.'

'True. I might just do that.' She laughed lightly, getting up and strolling slowly in the direction of the tennis court. 'I think I'll go and give the twins some tennis coaching. Something tells me they need it!'

And she needed a respite from well-meaning family interference, she acknowledged wryly, making her escape with a sense of relief. Searching out an old racket and battered white tennis pumps from the nearby garden shed, she joined the twins and found herself hauled into an exhausting game involving much chasing after their wildly hit tennis balls. Her pink and yellow floral summer dress with its dropped waist and long, flowing skirt had been a perfect choice for a family garden party, but was scarcely the correct attire for tennis, she soon realised. The twins cheekily suggested tucking the skirt up into her knickers, clutching each other in howls of laughter when Henrietta did exactly that and revealed long, lightly tanned thighs with smooth, well-proportioned muscles from years of being captain of Graystone Abbey's tennis team.

As the game grew sillier, and she grew flushed and out of breath, she began to feel a great deal better about her disastrous meeting with Nicholas Trevelyan. She'd just mentally consigned him to Siberia when her attention was caught by Piers waving to her from the court entrance.

'Hi, Hetti...come and see who I invited along as a surprise this afternoon!' Piers was laughing, slightly shamefacedly, and jerking his head behind him to where a tall newcomer had invaded the peaceful family group, exuding relaxed confidence as he accepted champagne and canapés from her mother, and talked easily with her father and Hugo. Henrietta stared incredulously, her heart beginning to thump unnecessarily fast. It wasn't...it couldn't be...

For a few seconds, she felt too angry to move, but then the man turned and looked towards her, and self-protection took over, as she suddenly realised what she must look like. Her stripey blonde hair had escaped its neat topknot, cascading wildly down her back, her face was flushed and hot, and her demure summer dress was tucked up in an extremely unladylike fashion.

She quickly pulled her dress down over her legs, and raked trembling fingers through her heavy mane of hair, heat creeping into her cheeks and prickling her neck.

She could hardly believe it, but Piers's surprise guest, the dark man currently centre-stage in the fair-haired Beauman party, like a devil among angels, was none other than the obnoxious Nick Trevelyan himself.

CHAPTER TWO

TALK seemed to be flowing easily among the group on the patio, and Nick Trevelyan appeared to be holding his own extremely well, demonstrating a skilled veneer of social charm. Watching his hard, bony face relaxed into laughter, Henrietta damped down an added spark of annoyance, recognising it as completely illogical. Why should she feel resentful if her family were being their usual friendly, welcoming selves? She'd just been wishing they weren't quite so over-protective of her, hadn't she? She would hardly have thanked them for descending on him with righteous indignation, berating him for daring to upset their beloved Henrietta!

Besides, a small voice nagged, he was Piers's boss, and, however cross she might feel with Piers right now, her brother couldn't have *known* how badly her interview would go. Presumably he must have invited Nick Trevelyan here tonight thinking he was being helpful, boosting her chances of getting a top job, and anyway, being downright rude to Nick Trevelyan certainly wouldn't do Piers's partnership ambitions any good...

So loyalty to her family urged caution as she approached the laughing group. A brief clash of personalities at an interview wasn't grounds to cut the person dead at the next meeting.

But being pleasant to Nick Trevelyan felt like the hardest thing she'd ever managed to do.

'I've topped up your champagne glass, darling!' Her mother was passing the tray around, smiling encour-

agingly at the gathered circle, and warningly at Henrietta.
'Let's welcome our unexpected visitor. And drink to the
twins—I simply can't believe it's ten years since they
shattered our peace and tranquillity!'

They all duly drank the toast, and the twins'
exuberance caused a welcome diversion from the circle
of eyes watching her reaction to the presence of their
uninvited guest.

'Hello again, Mrs Melyn.' The laughter had left the
green eyes as he turned to her, and the cool scrutiny she
was subjected to took in every detail of her appearance,
from the chaotic state of her hair, the beads of perspiration on the bridge of her short, lightly freckled nose,
down over the sleeveless floral dress clinging damply to
her breasts, finishing up with her dusty bare toes. 'Sorry
to gatecrash a family party.'

'You haven't. You're Piers's invited guest.'

'I'm also the last person you wanted to see this
evening. Right?'

The twist of mockery at the corner of his hard mouth
made her stare at him warily.

'Not at all, Mr Trevelyan. What on earth made you
think that?'

'Just a hunch.' He drank some champagne in a swift,
impatient movement and checked his watch, turning
away from her as Piers said something to him, leaving
her a few moments to inspect his rugged profile with
irresistible curiosity.

He looked different, tonight. The formal business suit
was gone, and he wore casual olive cords and a cream
and green checked shirt, open at the neck, revealing black
hair on a tanned chest. He seemed taller than ever. Maybe
it was because she was barefoot.

But his face looked different. He was more relaxed, perhaps. Yet he didn't look totally relaxed. The dark features looked permanently wary, even when he smiled, and his lean body seemed to radiate a kind of coiled tension. His face was deeply tanned, with deep-set eyes, a long nose, a firm wide mouth with a sensual lift to the upper lip, and an aggressive chin. The small scars, relics of that tragic car accident, gave him a slightly sinister air. Laughter lines fanned out from the corners of his eyes, though he didn't strike her as the jolly laughing type at all. If childhood memory didn't play her false, he might once have had a habit of laughing at the world beneath those heavy, deceptively sleepy eyelids, but she sensed that if there was indeed a nicer side to Nicholas Trevelyan these days she was unlikely to see much of it if she became an employee.

Confusion suddenly fogged her brain, and she sipped some more champagne, feeling the tiny bubbles tickling her nose. Was it possible, she wondered, to dislike someone intensely, yet be strangely drawn to them at the same time? She ought to stop drinking champagne and go in and make a pot of coffee, she told herself hazily, but she stood still, watching Nick Trevelyan as he discussed something with Piers, almost mesmerised by the way he moved his body and his hands as he talked.

'I think I'll get the twins to bed now, darling,' her mother confided, catching both Genevieve and Juliette by the hand and hauling them, protesting, towards the french doors. 'I won't be long!'

'I'll sort out these two, don't worry!' Henrietta swiftly deposited her glass on a nearby table, and prepared to take charge. Nick Trevelyan swung round, his eyes swiftly assessing the scene.

'Would you mind if I took your daughter out to dinner, Mrs Beauman? I'd like to discuss a couple of points arising from our interview today.'

'Not in the least!' Her mother beamed traitorously, avoiding Henrietta's impassioned eyes. 'I was just about to forbid her to help with the twins in any case. She does far too much. I think she'd clean the house and weed the garden if we didn't have a couple in who do it before she gets there!'

'Mother, really, I——'

'Nonsense, darling. Run along. Mrs Gowan can supervise this pair.'

'But I'm far too tired, in any case.' She was being appallingly ungracious, she knew, but panic had engulfed her. Go out to dinner with Nick Trevelyan? She'd rather sup with the devil!

'Off you go, Hett!' Piers put his arm round her and gave her a squeeze, blue eyes laughing. 'Wait till you see Nick's car——' he winked at the dark man observing the proceedings with a wry gleam in his eyes '—it's worth keeping awake a bit longer for, I promise you!'

Was there an element of hero-worship in Piers's attitude towards Nick Trevelyan? Henrietta decided irritably that there was. And it appeared there was nothing for it, she'd have to go. But she was simmering with temper as she collected bag and shoes, and spent two minutes in the bathroom rinsing her face and hands, dragging a brush ferociously through her hair, and applying a slick of gold eyeshadow and pink lipstick to salvage what she could of her appearance. As an afterthought, she fluffed some of her mother's Pierre Cardin talcum powder under her arms, and rinsed the dust off her bare feet in the bidet.

Slightly more composed, she rejoined everyone on the terrace, and bore the close scrutiny of Nick Trevelyan's green gaze yet again as he assessed her freshened appearance with mocking amusement.

'Shall we go?' he murmured softly.

Their feet crunched on the gravel as they rounded the vicarage to the wide courtyard at the side, where among the assortment of family cars a glossy dark green vintage sports car waited, its hood down to reveal plush cream leather seats.

'How attractive,' she commented, icily polite, as he opened the door for her.

'Would you like the hood up or down, Mrs Melyn?'

'Since I've abandoned all hope of securing my hair in a demure style, you might as well leave it down. It's a lovely evening.'

They drove in silence, up the steeply sloping series of hairpin bends leading from the church and vicarage and the tiny hamlet of St Wenna, and on to the cliff road which led through Trevelyan land, and eventually passed Trevelyan House, a large granite mansion in the distance. Old Hector Trevelyan had died recently, she remembered hearing from somewhere. Had Piers told her? Or her father, who would undoubtedly have conducted the funeral service? She was suddenly ashamed of how out of touch she was with local gossip. Too busy avoiding being the topic, she reflected wryly, even though it was nearly four years since the scandal and rumour surrounding Tristan and herself.

'According to my secretary, Gillian,' he said at last, as they began the steep descent into the tiny fishing cove of Trebarnock, 'you're the best bilingual secretary I'm likely to get this far from London.'

She glanced at him, astonished by the apparent frankness of his words, and by the fact that he'd paid her a compliment. Then the nature of the compliment filtered through, and she grimaced. That was a classic backhander, if ever she heard one. Implying that because they lived in the wilds of Cornwall, he had to make the best of a poor choice!

'I disagree with her,' he added, pulling the Alvis into the car park of the notoriously expensive Trebarnock Cove Hotel, and cutting the engine. 'I think you're probably the best bilingual secretary I could find, period.'

'Really?' She swallowed hard as the pale gaze flicked over her, trying to assess this sudden change in tactics. Was he trying to charm her? If so, she was in dire peril of succumbing. Take a grip on yourself, she lectured silently. The man was a Jekyll and Hyde.

'This is rather sudden, Mr Trevelyan. What are you basing your opinion on? Those three letters I typed?'

'Gillian confirmed you did them in record time, with no errors, and no discarded copies. You'd even corrected my deliberate errors. Full marks.' His tone was even, as he got out and came round to open her door, overwhelming her with a punctilious display of courtesy. 'Let's go and talk about it over dinner.'

Climbing out and following him into the hotel, she couldn't help suddenly seeing the funny side. Was this really the 'fearsome Trevelyan' as Piers called him, wining and dining her, paying her compliments? Caution was called for, a great deal of it, she decided. Nicholas Trevelyan might be making an effort at the moment, but she suspected it was a calculated routine to get what he wanted. He'd shown a distinct aptitude for being boorish and obnoxious, but worse still he exuded some aura of confident control she found unnervingly attractive. In fact, he was just the kind of male she found most threatening.

The dining-room overlooked Trebarnock Cove, with its shingled inlet strewn with seaweed and fishing boats, nestling in the curved stone arm of the harbour wall. Henrietta's eyes kept straying to the evening activity on the quayside, anything to evade Nick Trevelyan's probing, heavy-lidded gaze across the pink-clothed table. Sipping the glass of Perrier she'd requested, she tried hard to be decisive about the menu.

'Also according to my secretary, Gillian, who I suspect is gaining in courage because she's leaving, I didn't make a favourable impression on you at the interview today. In fact, she told me you came out of my office in quite a temper. What are you going to have to eat, Mrs Melyn?'

'I—er——' She focused frantically on the elegant Gothic print in the menu, totally thrown by his unexpected words. 'I'm sorry, I'm not feeling very decisive…'

'Then what about melon and prawns, followed by the chicken *cacciatore*?'

She stiffened, illogically annoyed by his accurate stab at her tastes. 'No. I'll have the pâté, please, and then——' she glanced rapidly down the menu '—and then the wild duck with mushrooms.'

She ignored the sudden gleam of amusement in his eyes, relieved when the head waiter hurried across to greet Nick like an old friend, while another waiter, presumably of less importance, hovered behind him to note down her choice with a flourish on his notepad. Nick requested home-made minestrone followed by *boeuf stroganoff* and wild rice, then turned his attention to the wine waiter.

'No wine for me, thank you,' Henrietta said politely. The champagne had already taken its toll. She'd better keep a clear head from now on. Nick Trevelyan scanned the extensive wine list briefly before adding a half-bottle of Cabernet Sauvignon and a bottle of mineral water to the order.

'So...presumably taking me out to dinner tonight was your secretary Gillian's idea of making amends, Mr Trevelyan?' she queried drily, when they were finally alone.

'No. This was my idea.'

'A very spur of the moment idea, then. Unless you *knew* for certain I'd be at the vicarage tonight?'

'When Piers mentioned a family birthday party it wasn't too far-fetched to expect to find you there.'

'I hadn't realised you were particularly friendly with Piers, outside office hours that is...'

'All right, I confess. Piers's invitation tonight came as a bit of a surprise. But my motive for accepting was to see you again, just as I suspect Piers made the suggestion knowing it would coincide with our interview earlier...' The cool, detached tone of voice robbed these words of any trace of intimacy, but she swallowed awkwardly, suddenly feeling absurdly shy in his company.

'Plus your brother and I do have a recent shared interest, I suppose,' Nick went on, 'outside of estate agency...'

'Shared interest?' She frowned, trying to make the connection and distracted by the growing sensation of being manipulated, either by Piers, or by Nick Trevelyan, or both...

'Flying.' He smiled slightly at her raised eyebrows. 'Piers is a recent convert to light aircraft—he's started taking flying lessons.'

This was news to Henrietta, so presumably it must be a *very* recent departure—Piers wasn't likely to keep such an exotic new hobby a secret for long.

'So...?'

'So he's keen to tag along as often as possible on my cross-Channel hops in a Cessna 172.'

'Oh, I see—you've got your own plane?'

He nodded briefly, his eyes cool, almost wary.

'What triggered your interest in flying?'

He shrugged slightly. 'Who knows? Maybe the *inaccessibility* of it?'

'You mean you wanted the challenge?'

The green eyes seemed to harden slightly at her continued probing.

'Possibly...or the freedom. Don't you ever wish you could escape from various situations, Mrs Melyn?'

'I wish you'd stop calling me that!' she said abruptly, finding the mocking form of address unbearable all of a sudden. There was a brief, charged pause, and then Nick Trevelyan leaned slightly back in his chair, watching her carefully, like a large cat weighing up the vulnerability of its prey.

'What would you like me to call you?'

The expression in his narrowed eyes made her self-conscious, and she fidgeted with her heavy rose damask napkin, unravelling it from its folds and spreading it on her lap.

'I...I don't know! I'm sorry, Mr Trevelyan. I don't know why I said that. I'm tired and tense. It's been rather a long day...'

'Would you prefer me to call you Henrietta?'

There was a soft, unfathomable note in his voice. Somehow he managed to make something as simple as her own name sound like a daring intimacy. Unexpectedly she blushed deeply. She had the unnerving sensation of plunging into murky, dangerous waters.

'Well, all this formality does seem rather overdone.' She shrugged slightly, wishing he'd take his eyes off her, stop gazing at her face with that impassive, piercing scrutiny. 'I'm quite happy for you to call me Henrietta.'

'In that case you'd better call me Nick. At least, while we're having dinner. I prefer formality in the office.'

'That's assuming I agree to work for you.'

'I'm offering you the job as my personal secretary.'

Why did it feel as if he was constantly mocking her? His expression was deadpan, now, his eyes bland.

'I . . . I'd like a little longer to think about it . . .'

Nick Trevelyan's expression barely altered, but his jaw tightened. Here was a man who didn't like being crossed, she reflected with a shiver of apprehension. Something about him, some detail from the past, something connected with his brother's death in that car accident, was niggling at the back of her mind, and she wished she could remember what it was. With the vicarage land adjoining Trevelyan land, and Nick's friendship with Tristan's older brother Giles, their affairs had overlapped at various intervals, but in the circumstances it was surprising how little she actually knew about him. Maybe it was because of the age-gap. She'd always known who he was, and that chance encounter on the cliffs, by Trebethick Mill, when Sammy got trapped, had stayed in her mind with peculiar clarity.

But she'd been so much younger. And while Nick Trevelyan's peer group included Giles, they'd been away at boarding-school, and then gone off to pursue their careers. She had still been a child while he was a young man away in London studying music.

Music! That was it. The past came flooding back, surprising her with its intensity. That Christmas party at the Melyns', when she'd been fifteen, and Nick Trevelyan had been there, so changed from the kind, laughing man on the horse the previous summer, cold and remote, his face and hand bearing the fresh scars of the aftermath of the car crash, when his brother Bevan had been killed. The rumour circulated that Nick had been forced to give up his place at the London Academy because of his injuries. Presumably he'd stepped into Bevan's shoes, taken over the family firm of auctioneers and estate agents, as his father must have wanted him to...

'Eat your pâté, Henrietta.' The deep voice startled her back to the present, and she glanced down at the table, realising that while she'd been staring pensively out of the window their first courses had arrived.

'Excuse me...I was miles away...'

'I could see that. And something tells me you weren't even thinking about my offer.'

'Your offer?'

'The job offer,' he prompted patiently, the pale green eyes flickering with sarcasm. 'Though I'm beginning to wonder if I want a secretary who can't even concentrate on a conversation over the dinner table!'

'No...I'm sorry... Actually, I was thinking about what you said at the interview earlier this evening. About how time changes people...'

Nick Trevelyan's eyes narrowed slowly, but he said nothing, his silence forcing her to blunder on.

'I...I was wondering if you ever play the violin now.'

His soup spoon was halfway to his mouth, and he carefully lowered it back to his dish, and the pause which followed lengthened into an endless void, leaving

Henrietta increasingly aware that she'd stumbled into a vetoed area.

'No. I hardly ever play the violin now. What made you think of that?' The deep voice was coldly controlled.

'I . . . oh, the twins are having lessons at the moment. They're not very good yet. The whole village echoes with the agonised screeching! But, just . . . meeting you again today. I suddenly remembered hearing you play at a Summer Music Festival in Bodmin, years ago—we all went along to listen to Piers performing on the piano, and then we had to wait until Helen's age group came on, so we could hear her flute recital, and your section came in between. I can't have been more than about . . . nine! I was really annoyed because I wasn't allowed to bash out "I Can Sing a Rainbow" on my glockenspiel.'

'I recall you had a good singing voice, though. I came with Giles to that folk club in Wadebridge once or twice. You used to sing and play the guitar, am I right?'

'Well, yes.' For some reason she felt warmth creep into her cheeks. 'Tristan and I used to go there quite a lot...he just liked listening to folk music...but he always said I had a dreadful voice! And my guitar playing was limited to five basic chords!'

Nick Trevelyan was looking at her strangely. 'That's not how I recall it. I've a clear recollection of you singing a stirring rendition of "One Misty Moisty Morning", and practically getting a standing ovation. Another musical Beauman, I remember thinking.'

'Well, they say music is Cornwall's traditional art form...and anyway Piers was the most talented,' she said hurriedly. 'Though he hardly ever plays the piano now. He's too busy charging around the country, pursuing his "yuppy" lifestyle...'

'Your brother Piers has a lot to learn,' Nick said dismissively, making her glance at him in slight surprise. 'But you're right, the Cornish are traditionally musical.'

'But none of us could hold a candle to you!' Her reserve was momentarily forgotten in a warm flash of memory. 'That festival almost ground to a halt when you came on stage and played those Celtic folk tunes!'

There was a silence then.

'What excellent memories we both appear to have, Henrietta.'

Nick Trevelyan finished his soup, his eyes unfathomable again as he glanced across at her. 'Perhaps Gillian's character assessment was sound after all. A good memory is one of the things I look for in a secretary.'

They were back to the subtle put-downs again, she reflected, a reminder of who they both were and why they were having dinner together, and with a touch more colour in her cheeks she finished her pâté in silence.

'Tell me about this French grandmother of yours,' he invited at length, as the main course was placed in front of them, and he politely passed her the platter of exquisitely cooked baby sweetcorn, courgettes and carrots. She helped herself to some of each, her eyes straying to the lean brown hand supporting the dish, finding herself unable to drag her gaze away from the deep jagged scar across the back of the knuckles, presumably where the wound must have sliced across all the tendons of his fingers. Realising he was watching her, she blinked away the sudden ache of sympathy she'd been experiencing, and obediently launched into an account of her grandparents' house near La Rochelle, her regular childhood visits there during her school holidays.

'Do you know Brittany?' The interruption was cool, and she realised she'd been chattering on for too long. What was the matter with her? She didn't normally lose her composure like this, natter on heedlessly just for the sake of avoiding another charged silence.

'Yes, quite well. We've had family holidays there——'

'I'm attending a conference there, next weekend. I need a secretary to accompany me.'

'Next weekend? But...surely, Gillian...?'

'Gillian has picked next Saturday as her wedding-day.' The wide mouth grimaced with a trace of humour. 'So, while it's damned inconvenient, I decided to allow her the time off.'

'I see. You're asking *me* to come?'

Seeing her horrified reaction, his expression took on a glint of genuine humour, for the first time.

'I'm hardly suggesting you embark on a mission into outer space. Just a short flight to France, and a half-day conference to attend. Naturally I'll pay you well.'

She opened her mouth to refuse, then shut it again slowly. They had finished their main courses, and the waiter was back, with the dessert menu. Nick Trevelyan was waiting politely while she stared at the tempting selection.

'I'll have the charlotte russe, please.' She suddenly felt more decisive, more in control. She'd come to a decision, and it had more to do with taking positive action over her own life than with the insidious spell weaving itself around her in this man's company tonight.

'Bring me some of the trifle, please,' Nick said, handing the menus back to the waiter, 'and a pot of coffee...do you like cream, Henrietta?'

'Please.'

When the waiter had gone, Nick continued to hold her gaze, his lidded stare curiously compelling.

'Well? Will you help me next weekend, Henrietta?'

She nodded, expelling her breath sharply, surprised by the brief flash of triumph she thought she saw in his eyes. She wasn't sure what she was letting herself in for, but caution had been an integral part of her life for too long. Why not go? Why not take on the stimulus of this new job, for a man she didn't quite trust, didn't even like, but who seemed to have the knack of colouring her grey, rather introspective existence, of bringing everything vividly back to life again?

'You'd better let me have a full itinerary,' she advised him calmly, as they emerged a little later into the darkness and climbed into the sports car.

'Of course. Gillian will be in touch. Shall we put the hood up?'

She had a sudden premonition of how she'd feel, sitting so near to Nick Trevelyan in the enclosed intimacy of the car's interior, and shook her head quickly.

'No, leave it down again. It's not raining!'

'So hardy!' he murmured, feeling in the glove pocket and extracting a silk headsquare. 'The wind's stronger now. Put this over your hair, or you'll never get a brush through it in the morning!'

'No, I'm fine, honestly.' The sight of the silk Hermès scarf had produced an odd, unpleasant contraction inside her stomach, and she took a firm grip on her emotions. It was none of her business how many silk scarves he kept for the various women who must ride as passengers in his car. If she was going to let her imagination start running away with her, if she was going to let Nick Trevelyan's private life bother her, she'd better change her mind quickly about the job, and run a mile.

'Are you sleeping at the vicarage tonight?'

'No...but I need to go back there to get my car.'

He glanced at his watch, frowning slightly. 'Your address is in Hone, if I remember?'

'Yes—I rent a bedsit in Wharf Street.' She suppressed a sudden yawn, and glanced at him apologetically. 'Sorry, it's been a long day...' Another yawn was welling up, and she frantically tried to control herself. She suspected it was a reaction to the strange tension of the dinner with Nick Trevelyan, but even so it was hardly the politest way of ending the evening.

'It'll take ten minutes from here to Hone, and half an hour if we detour back to St Wenna and you have to drive yourself all the way from there. I'll take you to Hone, and pick you up in the morning when you want to collect your car.'

'Oh, no, I couldn't possibly expect you to do that!'

'There isn't a problem.' The subject appeared to be closed, and, feeling overpowered, she sat back with a slight shrug and gave in. She was too sleepy to argue. Tomorrow was Saturday, so there would be no rush. And the thought of driving her ancient Fiat all the way back from St Wenna, negotiating that steep narrow hill and all those hairpin bends, didn't exactly appeal at this time of night. She closed her eyes, and relaxed, and let the forward movement of the car force her head back against the head-rest, letting the night air flow wildly through her hair, the scent from the sea, and the cliff-top bracken and the sea-pinks spicing the cooler air.

When the motion of the car slowed, then stopped, she opened her eyes, momentarily confused. Then she saw Nick Trevelyan's dark face, thrown into gaunt relief beneath the dim light of the street-lamp, and she sat up straighter, embarrassed at falling asleep in his car. He'd stopped outside Number Twelve Wharf Street, and had half turned in his seat, one arm along the ledge of the driver's door, the other resting along the back of her seat. For a moment she had the idiotic notion that he was about to lean across and kiss her, and then she saw the mocking gleam in his eyes and she blushed hotly in the darkness, astonished at herself.

'Is this where you live?'

'Yes. Thanks very much, Ni . . . Mr Trevelyan . . .'

His mouth twisted wryly. 'We're not in the office yet.' He glanced up at the bleak, terraced house, which was in an area more famous for its links with the local slate quarry than for its outstanding natural beauty. 'This is a far cry from your parents' country vicarage. Is this all Tristan left you with?'

She stiffened, fumbling for the door handle and failing to find it. 'Tristan didn't leave me with anything.'

'You must have lived somewhere during your marriage.'

'His parents bought us a house,' she supplied woodenly, wishing she could find the correct catch to secure her escape. 'When Tris died I didn't consider I was entitled to anything.'

'Why didn't you go back home?'

'Is this vital information for the character assessment, Mr Trevelyan?'

'No. I'm just curious, Mrs Melyn.'

'I didn't go back home because, having chosen independence, I opted to stick to it.'

'But your family didn't agree.' It was more of a statement than a query. She inclined her head slowly.

'They weren't happy. We compromised for a short time. While I enrolled at secretarial college and finished my course, I lived at home. When I got my first job, I rented a room of my own.'

'And you've been here ever since?'

'Here? Good heavens, no. I've moved up-market coming to Wharf Street,' she said lightly. 'The first house I rented a room in was practically condemned for demolition!'

'And your parents allowed it?'

She met his narrowed gaze very steadily. 'I make my own decisions, Mr Trevelyan. I run my own life. My family respect that.'

His expression was unfathomable as he stared back at her. 'Freedom to learn by your own mistakes. Background support if you fall flat on your face?' he said thoughtfully. 'That kind of freedom can be worth any number of disasters. You don't know how fortunate you are, Mrs Melyn.' He got out to unfasten her door, looming very tall and intimidating above her as she swung her legs out. Self-consciousness made her clumsy. Her heel caught in the hem of her floaty summer dress, and she stumbled, with an ominous ripping sound, and almost sprawled full length on the pavement. Nick Trevelyan made a swift lunge and caught her easily by her arms, steadying her while she extricated the heel from her hem, holding her close enough for her to feel the heat radiating from his lean body, and suddenly breathless she raised a hot face to meet his level scrutiny.

'You were saying about falling flat on my face?' She laughed, lightly. His hands felt hard and firm on her bare arms, and they both seemed to suspend movement, frozen in the brief, intimate tableau. Cool green eyes locked with warm brown, and a subtle challenge seemed to hang in the air between them.

'Sometimes we all need a little extra support, Mrs Melyn.' He released her as suddenly as he'd grabbed her, and she swayed slightly, strangely shaken, shivering as he moved away from her and the cool night air surrounded her again. 'What time shall I call for you in the morning?'

'About eleven?' she suggested, more in consideration for his own Saturday morning routine than her own. Lie-ins were not something she included in her itinerary.

'Fine. I'll see you here at eleven. Goodnight…Henrietta.' His smile was a flash of white against the darkness of his face, and she responded involuntarily, the treacherous core of warmth returning to her stomach as she dug around for the key in her handbag.

'Goodnight, Nick.'

He waited until she'd let herself safely into the house, and appeared in her own upstairs window to draw the curtains, before driving away. And, tired as she was, Henrietta lay awake for what seemed like hours, turning over the events of the day in her mind.

CHAPTER THREE

ANY lingering air of magic from the evening out with Nick Trevelyan was abruptly dispersed when he called for her as promised. Her brilliant smile and breezy 'Good morning' was countered with the cold, assessing gaze she recognised from the interview, combined with a curt nod. Having woken to brilliant sunshine and an unaccountable mood of well-being and anticipation, Henrietta climbed into the sleek Alvis feeling crushed. The drive to St Wenna was endured in silence, broken only by the regular bleeps of the car phone and Nick Trevelyan's concise but ill-humoured handling of the incoming calls.

By the time they arrived at the vicarage, she was stiff with hurt pride, and battling very hard to stop herself from asking what was wrong with him. Just in time, she reminded herself that she had absolutely no right to ask him any such thing. He might have taken her out for dinner last night, and mellowed fractionally towards the end of the evening, but it had all been for ulterior motives. It hadn't been a social event. He'd wined and dined her as a businessman would wine and dine a useful contact he wanted to utilise to his advantage. Now he'd got what he wanted, and probably regretted the hassle of honouring last night's promise about the lift . . .

And *besides*, she lashed herself impatiently, *surely* she wasn't suddenly so gullible, so—so *deluded*, that she could crave the friendship of an arrogant devil like Nick Trevelyan? On a professional footing, she felt confident that she could handle him. But as far as personal relationships went...glancing over at his powerful profile, she recognised with a jolt what it was about him that had made her toss and turn so much in bed last night. He exuded...that domineering maleness, that masculine machismo...He embodied everything she actively avoided in a man...

But a job was a job, she reasoned calmly. And besides, there was that irresistible salary, which she frankly admitted would come in very handy. Plus, of course, this particular job would be challenging, and exciting, and exactly what she was trained for.

Taking a firm grip on herself, she turned a cool face towards him as they halted in the vicarage courtyard, realising that he'd abandoned the car phone and had just asked her a question.

'Sorry?'

'Have you decided to hand in your notice?' His tone was measured, impersonal.

'Yes, I accept the job, Mr Trevelyan,' she murmured politely, feeling his narrowed gaze on her jean-clad thighs as she climbed out of the car. 'Subject to written confirmation.'

'There'll be a letter in the post early next week.'

'Fine. And you'll let me know the form for next weekend?'

'I'll be in touch.' There was a twist of humour around his mouth, as he took in her bland-faced formality. But his eyes were cold as he backed the car, and lifted a hand in brief farewell before disappearing out of the gates, and Henrietta was glad of the excuse to pay another visit to the cheerful atmosphere of the vicarage to quash the infuriating twinge of dismay she felt at his going.

The rest of the week was spent tipping from one mood to another, like a see-saw. The typed job offer from Trevelyan Estates flopped on to her landlady's doormat on Tuesday morning, and she duly gave a month's notice to her current employers, who accepted it with the fatalistic air of a firm who were no longer in control of their staff. Since being taken over by a big nationwide banking consortium, they'd found themselves weighed down with memos and regulations from the faceless bureaucrats at head office, most of whom had as much idea of the land and estate agency business as they had of inter-galactic space exploration via satellites. They'd love to offer her more money and entice her to stay, they assured her wistfully, but the new rigid salary structures decreed otherwise.

Henrietta wasn't sorry to leave. Apart from the increasingly boring nature of the work, with its influx of pointless inter-office paperwork, and petty restrictions, some of the girls in the typing pool had looked out an old copy of a national newspaper's gossip column. They had discovered to their delight that Henrietta had a past worthy of regular secret gossips in the ladies' cloakroom, to be abruptly ceased only when Henrietta herself walked in to a sudden, pointed silence. Having endured several months of this, and since a similar thing had happened at her previous job, the prospect of a respite was welcome.

'You're quite sure you're happy about going off on this French weekend with Nick Trevelyan?' Helen probed, appearing on a rare visit on Wednesday night bearing an expensive bottle of Hock, a dish of salad, a French stick, and a home-roasted cold chicken stuffed with fresh tarragon.

'Quite happy!' Henrietta examined the contents of Helen's basket and laughed. 'And why do I get the feeling I'm in for a sisterly lecture?'

'Whatever gives you that impression?'

'Whenever you come bearing lavish gifts, you're normally on a family-sent mission to check I'm OK!' Henrietta teased, flicking a fresh green and white checked tablecloth over the round table under the window, and placing the food and wine in pride of place in the centre. 'Isn't Hugo on call tonight?'

'Well, yes, he is. But I've left my housekeeper in charge of the phone.' Helen had the grace to look slightly shamefaced. 'I confess I wanted to talk to you, Hetti. But don't feel you've got to serve up the chicken now, darling! I intended it as a boost to the usual diet of baked beans and jacket potatoes you seem addicted to!'

'Since I've only just got back from the swimming-baths, and I haven't had supper yet, and since I'm going away for the weekend, we might as well enjoy this right now!' Henrietta occupied herself with polishing her only two wine glasses and tackling the mysteries of the cork-screw with a skill acquired through necessity.

'He's got quite a reputation, Hetti.'

Henrietta marvelled at her own composure, as she paused only fractionally in the act of pulling the cork out, her face averted from her older sister's.

'Who has?'

'You know quite well who I'm talking about. Nick Trevelyan. I was listening in when Piers was talking about him the other night.'

Henrietta began a lengthy search for the salad servers, glad that she had left her hair down after swimming, so that its heavy curtain hid her flushed cheeks. She reflected privately that Helen's proneness to interfering in other people's business, while always well-meaning, could become seriously annoying.

'I presume you mean he's got a reputation with women? My last boss was renowned as a wicked womaniser! Is there something I ought to know about working for men like that, Helen? Something I've not come across until now?'

'It was the way he was looking at you, the other night...and the way you were looking at him, if it comes to that! You have to admit, he is terribly attractive, and besides——'

'He was looking at me with a view to persuading me to work for him, Helen,' Henrietta cut in coldly. 'And if I remember correctly, I was looking at him thinking I heartily disliked him. I don't find him attractive...' She bit her lip, avoiding Helen's eyes. That was a little white lie, and she couldn't pretend otherwise. She *had* noticed Nick Trevelyan was attractive, in a completely objective way, of course. She wasn't sure exactly when she'd noticed. Possibly towards the end of their dinner together...

'I can see some women might find him irresistible,' she conceded, lightly, 'but personally I don't go for the dark, brooding type. Was that all you wanted to say?'

Her sister sighed. 'Sorry, darling. Piers made a comment the other night, that's all. And then Mother and I——'

'Don't tell me! You and Mother started worrying that I'd gone out to dinner with him, and *he* drove me back to get my car the following morning? You think I spent the night with him?'

'No, I didn't think that,' Helen said quickly. 'I think I know you better than that!'

'Quite. One-night stands aren't exactly my style.'

There was a very long pause, their eyes locked, both remembering the past without any need to speak the thoughts aloud.

'Did you ever tell Mother what happened between you and Tristan, Hetti?'

Henrietta took a sip of wine, and passed the basket of bread, her face a mask, her heart thumping violently at the unexpected line of attack. 'No. I only told you...' And Clare Harvey, she recalled. Clare had been a good friend since schooldays, bridesmaid at her wedding, and right up until Tris's death, when she'd come home to Cornwall and Clare had stayed on in London to pursue her modelling career, they'd kept in regular contact. She'd told part of it to Clare...

'Helen, Mum and Dad warned me about Tris, but I didn't take any notice! Do you think I wanted to give them more ammunition to say "I told you so" with? Wasn't Tristan's *death* enough?'

'I always thought they handled it wrong,' Helen said thoughtfully. 'If they hadn't tried to forbid you to see Tristan, you'd never have rushed into that silly marriage—you were going through an awkward stage; your nose was put out of joint over the twins. They virtually drove you into Tris's arms, if you want my opinion. You'd have come to your senses if they'd only given you time to work things out for yourself!'

Helen saw the flash of cool rebellion in the younger girl's eyes, and stopped.

'Helen, stop talking about me as if I were one of your educational psychology subjects, will you, and eat your supper?'

Helen studied her younger sister's determined levity at length, and finally appeared to abandon the topic, and Henrietta breathed a silent sigh of gratitude. She'd long had occasion to regret letting her heart rule her head over Tristan Melyn, and after the initial confiding in her sister she'd made it a policy never to let herself be drawn on the subject in any depth ever again. It certainly wasn't a policy she wanted to abandon at the moment.

They lapsed into silence while they ate, and Henrietta gave herself up to the unaccustomed pleasure of two excellent meals within one week.

'So...do you want all the gossip on Nick Trevelyan?' Helen prompted, when they'd consumed healthy quantities of chicken and salad and made a sizeable dent in the French stick.

'You know how I feel about gossip.' Henrietta made a wry face as she spoke, to avoid appearing too pompous.

'Meaning you've been the subject of so much of it yourself? I phrased that badly, didn't I? I should have said, "Do you want the facts on Nick Trevelyan"?'!'

'Facts related second- or third-hand amount to the same thing as gossip, in my book.'

'Hetti...!' Helen gave her an exasperated glare, then sighed, shaking her head. 'You can be extremely stubborn at times! Did you know that?'

'Yes! In fact, I've always been told that I was extremely stubborn *all* the time. I must be improving. Do you want some more wine?'

'Not if I'm driving. In fact, I'd better be going, Hett.' Helen stood up ruefully, bestowing a glance of grudging admiration on her younger sister. 'Apologies for the interfering big-sister act.' Helen collected her now empty basket and light summer jacket from the chair, and gave her a searching look as she kissed her cheek. 'But you've had your share of bad luck, darling. You know how we all worry about you!'

'Don't I just!' Henrietta suppressed the urge to scream, and hugged Helen warmly as she saw her to the door. 'And you can sleep easy in your beds, Helen. Nick Trevelyan can dabble in the white slave trade in his spare time, for all I care. It's of no interest to me. My contract states that I'm about to become his extremely well-paid personal assistant, and that, I promise, is the full extent of my involvement!'

This positive announcement bolstered her flagging morale over the next couple of days. Reiterated mentally at regular intervals, it lulled her into a false sense of security which crumbled abruptly the moment Nick Trevelyan called to collect her, shortly after dawn, the following Saturday morning.

'Did you receive my itinerary, Mrs Melyn?' The cool green eyes assessed her neat French plait, impeccable navy suit and minimal luggage with reluctant approval as she walked out to the car.

'Yes. It came on Thursday morning.'

'Good. So I can rely on you to keep everything running smoothly, can I?'

She glanced at him levelly as he stowed her small handgrip in the boot and climbed into the Alvis beside her.

'Since I'm not actually working in your office yet, I can't take responsibility for the files you'll need, and for the hospitality arranged with your business contacts, but I assume Gillian's taken care of all that?'

'I'm assuming so, too.' The hard, oddly sensual mouth twisted wryly. 'Although with Gillian's preoccupation with her groom-to-be, I suspect anything could happen.'

'As long as any mix-ups don't go down as a black mark on *my* future references!'

'You are ambitious, aren't you, Mrs Melyn?'

'I don't recall trying to hide the fact, Mr Trevelyan.'

They appeared to be back on formal name terms, she reflected, and the cutting sarcasm, the mocking note he'd utilised to devastating effect during their interview, was back with a vengeance. It was as if he was determined to keep her at arm's length, even at the expense of simple civility. Well, that suited her perfectly, didn't it? She wasn't exactly ripe for close friendship with the opposite sex herself.

But, nevertheless, she found herself wishing she'd allowed Helen to fill her in on Nick Trevelyan's mysterious 'reputation'. Noble though it might have been, her refusal to listen to gossip meant she didn't really have any idea what she was letting herself in for this weekend.

They were heading for the airport, and Henrietta leaned back in her seat, working hard on her much-practised relaxation techniques. There was a certain amount of normal tension involved at the start of a weekend like this, but her strung-up feelings far outstripped the norm. She hated to admit it, but Nick Trevelyan had a disturbing effect on her equilibrium.

Maybe it was because she was unsure of her ground with him. One minute he seemed friendly, the next minute aloof and scornful. Or maybe it was simply because the hood was up, and she was confined in the claustrophobic space of the car beside a surprisingly casual boss who was wearing Reeboks, tight, faded denims, open-necked rough denim shirt, and chunky tan leather flying jacket. He even had a night's growth of stubble, she detected, dismayed. The raw masculinity he emitted was decidedly unnerving. Helen's vague warnings lurked darkly at the back of her mind.

'We've missed the airport turn,' she pointed out suddenly, as the Alvis sped along the main road.

'We're flying from Huntsfield Aerodrome.'

'Huntsfield...oh! In your private plane, you mean?'

'Correct. Sorry, didn't I make that clear?' There wasn't a trace of apology in the mocking glance he angled at her, and she gritted her teeth in grim apprehension.

The four-seater Cessna turned out to be a small blue and grey aircraft, parked in the early morning sun among an assortment of other light aeroplanes on a stretch of grass beside the runway, looking barely big enough to rate toy status. She rapidly realised that if she'd found Nick's close proximity in the Alvis claustrophobic, her nerves would be at screaming pitch in the minuscule interior of the Cessna.

'Can this tiny plane really fly all the way to France?' Her light laugh didn't quite hide the stirrings of panic. Nick paused in his methodical check-over of what seemed to be every nut, bolt and hinge of the aircraft, and shot her a shrewd glance.

'You've never flown in a plane this size before?'

'No. And I can't think why you're looking so surprised. I wouldn't think many people have!'

He inspected her tense face with scant sympathy. 'I'll be selling this soon, to get a six-seater Cessna 411. One of your jobs as my secretary will be escorting parties of prospective buyers on inspection trips to Brittany. So if you've got a flying phobia, get rid of it fast!'

He turned and strode off in the direction of the control tower, leaving her standing uncertainly beside the aircraft, seething with indignation.

'Thank you very much!' she muttered when he returned a few minutes later, took her bag and stowed it in the rear luggage compartment with his, and prepared to help her up into the passenger-seat, a high step up which caused the tight, knee-length skirt of her business suit to ride to mid-thigh.

'You could have warned me to wear trousers!' she added hotly, silently cursing the high-heeled court shoes which only aggravated her dilemma.

'What, and spoil my early morning entertainment?' Nick's amusement was palpable as he reached over her bare tanned thighs, impervious to her efforts to straighten her skirt, and clipped the lap-strap of her seatbelt in place. She was crimson-faced when he leaned even further across her, sliding the shoulder harness from its hook and buckling it across her breasts, with brief instructions on how to tighten and loosen it.

'Sorry if I appear to be getting intimate.' He grinned callously, inspecting her heated appearance. 'But you need to be well strapped in.'

'I also have a pair of perfectly efficient hands, quite able to buckle straps all on their own!' she said unsteadily. 'So I'd be grateful if you'd stop being so *bloody chauvinistic*!'

He'd been about to slam her door, and he stopped, searching her irate face with that piercing gaze she found increasingly unnerving.

'Careful, Mrs Melyn. That's no way to talk to your new boss.'

'And that's no way to treat your new secretary!' she countered, taking a deep breath and trying to keep a sense of proportion. Was she angry at his cool impertinence, or at her own wild reactions to his touch? The casual brush of his hands against her legs and her breasts had brought her out in goose-bumps. She'd been ashamed to feel her nipples pull and tauten beneath the navy silk of her jacket. Her physical response had taken her totally by surprise, flustering and confusing her.

'Look,' she began, more calmly, 'as your personal secretary, I'll undertake to be polite and helpful at all times. I'd just appreciate it if you could try to treat me as an equal. Please don't patronise me, Mr Trevelyan.'

'You think I patronise you?' he said softly, after a very long pause.

'Well, yes...'

'Go on, Mrs Melyn.'

'Go on...?' Her throat was drying rapidly under the glittering challenge of his stare.

'Elucidate. You can't make accusations like that without backing them up with examples.'

She expelled her breath sharply. The man was insufferable.

'Your attitude at the interview last week was condescending. Then you took me out to dinner and managed to be passably pleasant. The next morning you virtually ignored me. It was all you could do to growl a greeting. This morning, you're treating me like some...some brainless bimbo, implying I'm practically witless just because I'm nervous of flying in a tiny little toy aeroplane for the first time in my life! At the risk of putting my new job in jeopardy, I simply can't imagine how your secretary Gillian has put up with you for so long...'

She stopped. A pulse was beating rapidly in her neck. She was aware that he'd become very still.

'Anything else?'

It was that deep, silky voice she remembered with a shiver from the interview.

'Yes. The way you keep calling me Mrs Melyn...'

'Ah, yes. You prefer Henrietta. Is this through a desire for greater intimacy, or a subconscious wish to forget

Tristan Melyn was ever unfortunate enough to marry you?'

The barb was softly ruthless. She caught her breath, biting her lip hard to retain the cool composure she'd started with.

'Neither.' She had no wish to be drawn into verbal fencing on the subject of Tristan. 'And in my opinion dragging this discussion down to the level of personal insult shows...shows lamentable immaturity!'

There was a resounding silence, and then Nick Trevelyan gave a short crack of astonished laughter, then began to laugh in earnest, as if she'd just told him a really funny joke. Henrietta was surprised at how contagious his laughter was. After his callous allusion to her marriage, she had no desire to laugh as well, but it was difficult not to join him. He had a deep, full-blooded laugh, and glancing reluctantly across she saw that his harsh features were totally transformed. The scars disappeared when he laughed. He lost that vaguely sinister air lent by those silver gouges against very dark skin.

'I can see you're going to be the most entertaining personal assistant I've ever had.'

'I wasn't actually *trying* to be entertaining...' She felt hot with indignation but her lips were twitching nevertheless.

'Then heaven help me when you are!'

He finally stopped laughing, and slammed her door firmly shut, sending unwelcome hormones scattering to every sensitive part of her body as he climbed in through the pilot's door and sat beside her.

'These planes definitely weren't designed for the larger figure!' she murmured lightly, attempting to cringe away sufficiently to sever contact between her arm and his, and giving up in defeat.

'True. You'll get used to it.' He was concentrating on flicking switches and checking gauges, clamping a set of headphones with mouthpiece on his head and handing an identical set to her, after more leaning over and plugging in somewhere in the region of her knees.

'Can you hear me all right?' His voice sounded disembodied, through the mouthpiece of the headphones. She nodded, adjusting her own set self-consciously. She was beginning to feel appalled at her violent outburst just now. Had she over-reacted to a spot of innocent manhandling by someone preoccupied and in a hurry?

Nick spoke rapidly to the control tower, and flicked some more switches. The engine noise rose, and Henrietta tensed in her seat. He flicked a wry glance towards her. 'Would it be patronising to point out there's a paper bag down beside your seat, in case of travel-sickness?'

'I never get travel-sick.'

'Fine. Well, it's a two-and-a-half-hour flight to Brittany. I suggest we pick a neutral topic and stick to it from now on. Agreed, *Henrietta*?'

His deliberate emphasis of her Christian name seemed designed to goad, but she kept the lid firmly on her temper.

'That sounds quite reasonable, Mr Trevelyan.'

'I suppose if I was trying to be really patronising, I'd insist you call me *sir*,' he said musingly. 'But since you're so set on casual intimacy between us, it had better be Nick.'

She suppressed a hasty retort. She'd said enough already, if she hoped to hang on to the job he was offering. And, besides, she was too intent on the strange experience of taking off, lifting effortlessly into the air in an aircraft so small and light a gust of wind might blow them all the way to France. After a few minutes, she was astonished to find she liked the sensation. Risking a peer out of the window, she could see the south-west peninsula of England spread out below, a hazy patchwork of fields and houses. With a strange elation, she felt a slight smile pull at the corners of her mouth, a completely involuntary response she couldn't hide. No wonder Piers was hooked—this was…it was… Descriptions failed her… It was a delight!

'All right?' Nick glanced across, his long green eyes tilting with amusement as he saw her entranced expression. 'I can see you are.'

'It's fun. I'm enjoying it.' She restrained herself from enthusing like a schoolgirl. She was here as his secretary, on a business trip, not as a friend on a fun day out.

'As soon as I can possibly afford it, I'm going to have a course of flying lessons!' she couldn't resist adding, with an incandescent smile which drew a long, hard stare from Nick.

'Are you serious?'

'Absolutely. Is there any reason why a mere female shouldn't learn to fly?'

'None whatsoever. But it doesn't come cheap, as I suspect your brother Piers is discovering!' His tone was dry, but his eyes were thoughtful as he turned back to the mysterious art of pulling levers and flicking more switches, and she sat back, unable to suppress the faint surge of excitement inside her, in spite of his dampening words.

The flight might have been two and a half hours, but it seemed far shorter. When she wasn't listening in, fascinated, to the constant crackle of voices over the radio headphones, and occasionally altering numbers, at Nick's instruction, on a small instrument called a transponder, they were discussing Trevelyan Estates and the aims of the coming weekend in Brittany. In spite of her lingering resentment at Nick's cavalier attitude towards her, by the time they landed on a small airstrip near Morlaix, Henrietta felt a lot wiser about his plans, and oddly excited at the prospect of working closely with him. He radiated a decisive, energetic optimism when he discussed business. It was refreshing after the apathy of her current employer.

'I think the latest fashion for selling out to big financial institutions is a mistake,' he told her reflectively. 'I've always favoured the lean and streamlined, but I want a broader European base. I'm negotiating a merger with a firm in Brest, with offices all over Brittany, and across into the Vendée.'

'It'll be hard keeping things lean and streamlined after the merger, won't it?'

'Not if I get the formula right. That's the point of all these negotiations. Mercier's set-up is similar to mine in size and approach. I've always moved fast, made snap decisions based on intuition. That's the style I want to keep. I think he does as well.'

'So you're getting the priorities established in black and white before signing anything?' She nodded approvingly as the small plane touched down surprisingly smoothly and taxied to a halt, glancing across as he turned to retrieve his leather jacket from the back. The movement brought him disturbingly close. She caught a whiff of cool masculine scent, some subtle combination like sandlewood soap and bergamot. She shivered slightly, reluctantly aware of how intimidatingly attractive he looked, with his short dark hair slightly tousled by the headphones on the flight.

'Precisely.' He grinned suddenly, affecting her shaky composure even more. 'I'm a great believer in sorting out the priorities. And number one priority right now is breakfast. What are the odds on finding a café serving coffee and croissants, Henrietta?'

'Fairly high, I should think.'

'Agreed. In fact there's a lovely old *auberge* on the way to Marc Mercier's farmhouse. I think it's called the *Ajoncs d'Or*. We'll go there.'

The local marshallers and *douaniers* had turned up to meet them on the Customs apron at the airstrip, checked their credentials and waved them on with an air of bored resignation. Just as Henrietta was about to ask if Gillian had organised transport from the airport, a sleek red BMW screeched to a flamboyant halt by the control tower and a black-haired, stocky, swarthy-skinned man jumped out, waving.

'Come and meet Marc Mercier,' Nick murmured drily, steering her towards the Frenchman, 'but bear in mind he's a lot more astute than he appears!'

She instantly understood what he meant. Marc Mercier projected a kind of charming ingenuity, but beneath the effervescent exterior and the friendly dark eyes she detected a shrewd, watchful intelligence.

'Do you mind if I drive, Marc?' Nick slanted the now familiar mocking eyebrow at the other man, who laughed good-naturedly, shaking his head.

'Not at all, not at all! Your English nerves cannot stand the pace at which I drive? *C'est vrai, n'est-ce pas?*'

'Quite true. I revel in some forms of excitement, but your driving is way above my tolerance levels, *mon vieux*.'

Without waiting for any possible show of chivalry, Henrietta opted for the back seat, and sat listening intently to the rapid conversation between the two men in the front, half in English, half in French. It appeared that Marc Mercier spoke excellent English, and Nick Trevelyan spoke excellent French. Her skills as an interpreter were hardly needed, she reflected with a stab of dismay. Why on earth had he insisted he needed her along this weekend?

After a while, Marc Mercier dispensed with business talk and leaned round to give his undivided attention to her as she sat silently in the back of the car.

'*Eh bien*, you are Nick's new personal secretary, *oui*?' The laughing black eyes made a rapid, thorough assessment of her face and figure, and she returned the scrutiny with polite composure. He subjected her to a volley of questions in swift French, and she responded with equal fluency.

'What a gem!' he exclaimed, turning back to Nick. 'Your new secretary speaks French like a native!'

'You approve?' Nick's tone was dry.

'I am enchanted!'

'I'm glad I've passed the test!' she murmured, with a half-laugh.

'*Mais, vraiment, madame,* you must tell me where you learned to speak such good French.'

Marc Mercier and Henrietta chatted animatedly in French from then on, while Nick drove the BMW with silent efficiency through maize and artichoke fields, past walnut trees and deep wooded valleys, and by the time they turned in at the crumbling grey stone gateposts of the *auberge* and swept to a halt in a flower-filled courtyard they were joking together like old friends.

'What excellent taste you have in secretaries, *mon vieux*!'

Nick's deadpan expression didn't alter, but Henrietta winced at the sledgehammer subtlety of the exuberant Frenchman.

'*Quel dommage* that she is married already!' he persisted, lifting her hand playfully to his lips and eyeing the gold band on her third finger. 'I might find a jealous husband when I come to take you out to dinner in England, *n'est-ce pas*?'

Henrietta stiffened, but mindful of the need for polite tolerance of her prospective boss's business contacts, she forced a light smile.

'Actually, I'm widowed. So if the dinner invitation arrives, I'll be delighted to accept, Monsieur Mercier!' It was an effort to ensure that her response was light and amused. Why on earth was she feeling so stiffly defensive? The man was only indulging in harmless flirtation. The kind you had to grit your teeth and bear for the sake of etiquette.

'Wonderful. It is a date, Henrietta! But widowed? So young? But this is terrible! This is devastating for you, *non*?'

As they took their seats at a table on the terrace, Henrietta caught Nick's eye. His deadpan expression was lit by a dark glitter of derision, and she felt a stab of surprise. Now what had she said or done?

'The resilience of human nature is remarkable,' he murmured drily, glancing over as a young girl hurried out to take their order. 'Life goes on, don't you agree, Henrietta?'

The undercurrent of mockery seemed so cruel that she wondered if she was becoming unduly sensitive, imagining stinging wounds where none had been inflicted.

'Quite right,' she retorted evenly. 'One can't wear widow's weeds forever.'

'Or in some cases, not at all?' The gibe was so soft and light, Nick's tone so bland, it was difficult to assimilate the scorching cynicism. 'What was it *Hamlet* observed? *"Frailty, thy name is woman"*?'

For a dreadful moment, she thought her eyes were going to fill with tears, but instead she controlled the pain with long-practised skill. But she was deeply shaken. Right from the first moment, when she'd walked into Nick's office for the interview, she'd sensed his underlying contempt. She'd discounted her qualms. She couldn't go through life seeing offence when it probably wasn't there. Self-confidence was a prize she'd slaved for, too valuable to throw away lightly.

But somehow Nick Trevelyan's opinion of her mattered more than most. Until now he'd kept it well-hidden beneath a cloak of mockery mixed with his own brand of cool reserve. But now here it was, disguised yet at the same time brazenly out in the open. He despised her. He despised her so thoroughly, he could even reveal it in front of his business colleague. Could she work for him, knowing that? Her pride stiffened, and she resolved to face up to the problem later, force a showdown if necessary. All the excitement and stimulation in the world, plus all the luxuries a super-salary would bring, wouldn't make up for blatant prejudice in her employer's attitudes.

'What will you have for *le petit déjeuner*, Henrietta?' The Frenchman's voice broke in on her thoughts, and she was jolted back to the present. He appeared oblivious to the undercurrents suddenly surfacing, or maybe he was too well-bred to comment?

She blinked away the introspective mood, and, squinting up into the sun, ordered *chocolat chaud* and *brioche au chocolat* with uninhibited anticipation.

Deliberately turning her back on Nick, she gave herself up to the uncomplicated ego-boost of Marc Mercier's apparent admiration.

CHAPTER FOUR

CROSSING one long, tanned leg over the other, Henrietta doodled idly on the edge of her notepad, trying her hardest to concentrate on the speaker addressing the gathering of French and English estate agents in the hotel. It seemed unusually warm for May. The navy suit felt too heavy for the oppressive atmosphere of the hotel, and she decided most of the other business-clad delegates must feel the same.

But the heat was only one reason for her lack of concentration. Her thoughts kept wandering off the subject, she acknowledged, and returning instead to Nick Trevelyan's barbed comments in front of Marc Mercier. Raw resentment still burned inside her, which probably accounted for her distinct lack of interest in the current proceedings, she reflected wryly. She wasn't at all sure she wanted to work for Nick Trevelyan any more, which gave her little inclination to operate willingly and efficiently on his behalf right now.

She fidgeted in her seat, and drew a picture of a square house with frilly lace curtains at all the windows in the corner of her notepad. For hours, it seemed, they'd been discussing myriad problems with the property market...commission rates, mortgage rates, planning regulations and development restrictions. It seemed endless, the topics requiring earnest debate. Taking the minimum of lucid notes was proving a feat of self-control. If she wasn't careful, she'd be scribbling reams.

'Shall we take a break?' Nick murmured in her ear, eyeing her doodles with a wry grin, his fingers closing round her upper arm as he steered her out into the hotel lobby. 'I don't know about you, but I'm desperate for a cup of tea, even if it's French tea!'

'After that gigantic lunch, I'm not sure I'll ever need to eat or drink again. But I agree, a cup of tea would be welcome,' she agreed coolly.

The pot of tea turned out to be very unEnglish-tasting, as expected, but refreshing.

'How's the note-taking going?' Nick enquired, his gaze bland over his cup. 'Will you be able to compile a report for me?'

'I imagine so.' She could probably manage to do that— before she informed him where he could stuff his precious job, she added silently. Carefully avoiding his eyes, she gazed around at the bustling hotel foyer, beyond the small salon where they were sitting, appraising the chic elegance of the French as they passed. Their fashion sense never failed to impress her; both the women and the men invariably looked so smart.

Although, since the transformation at Marc's farmhouse, Nick Trevelyan had to be a contender for the best-dressed man around, she reflected. The stubbled chin, the casual coarseness of denim and leather, had been supplanted by a dark charcoal-grey suit with an unmistakably loose designer cut to the jacket and softly pleated trousers, teamed with a pale grey and white striped shirt, and a silvery green silk tie. The tie went so well with Nick's cool, steel-green eyes she decided he must have chosen it specially. Vain, as well as conceited and insensitive, she told herself with bitter satisfaction. He looked every inch the successful European businessman. Her own chain-store outfit felt tawdry in comparison.

'Shouldn't we be in there, catching every word?' she suggested shortly, realising that he'd noticed her covert inspection of him. 'After all, you did fly over here specially for this conference!'

'Inaccurate. I flew over partly for this conference, and partly to further negotiations with Marc. The conference has exceeded its usefulness already. They covered the important points two hours ago. The rest is a lot of hot air.' He ran a finger around the collar of his shirt, as if he longed to be free of constriction.

'You're very sure of your facts!'

'I've had my say. Commission rates are the main bone of contention. They're a lot higher in France than in England, at present, as you probably gathered.'

'Did I hear you say in your speech that Marc actually organised this conference?'

'He and I instigated it. Why?'

'I was just wondering why, if your two firms are merging anyway... I mean, isn't this helping the competition?'

Nick laughed. 'Alas, Henrietta, Trevelyan Estates and Mercier Immobiliers do not have the sole rights to Anglo-French trading. Cornwall and Brittany have so many logical links. Look what's happening even more rapidly further along the coast, where the Channel is narrower. The Normandy agents are talking about doing over half their business with the British. It's inevitable here as well. A merger of great stealth and secrecy won't prevent dozens of other firms doing the same thing. The trick is to do it profitably!' He grinned at her suddenly, his teeth very white against his dark face, and Henrietta blinked involuntarily, taken unawares again by the potency of his charm when he chose to exert it.

'We'll have a lot of fun making our venture succeed and watching most of the others nose-dive,' he added, the flat assurance in the words belying any impression of boasting or over-confidence.

'We?' She couldn't resist it. Holding back her feelings for the sake of polite behaviour proved impossible any longer. 'I presume by "we", you mean you and Marc?'

The gaze grew more intent on her cool face, and Nick's eyes narrowed thoughtfully.

'I mean our two firms, with their respective employees. Which includes you, Henrietta.'

'No!' It was out, and there was nothing she could do to retract it. Foolish pride, she berated herself inwardly. This was the best job she'd ever find in Cornwall. So what? came the taut answer. Leave Cornwall, stop trying to prove something to yourself. You've proved once and for all it's not going to work, people are not prepared to give you the benefit of the doubt...

'No?' The cynical eyebrow had slanted, but his eyes darkened. 'You mean you're quitting, already? Before you've even started?'

'If that's how you want to describe it, yes.'

There was a deathly pause. She fidgeted uncomfortably with her teacup. At last, Nick leaned forward, his voice harsher. 'Henrietta, I think you should——'

'Neeck! Neeck, darling!' Whatever it was Nick had thought she should do was forgotten as a slender woman with long, shiny chestnut hair, beautiful as only a Frenchwoman could be beautiful, embraced him, Continental fashion, on either cheek, then grasped his shoulders and gazed reproachfully into his eyes. 'Marc told me you were coming over this weekend. *Ça va, cheri?* I've missed you, Neeck! *Mais, tu n'est pas gentil! Tu ne m'as pas téléphoné!*'

She perched herself on the arm of his chair, crossing her legs provocatively, letting one arm rest possessively along the chair back as she turned long, brilliantly blue eyes on Henrietta, with a faint, surprising gleam of hostility.

'Joelle.' It was impossible to tell whether Nick was pleased or bored by the woman's arrival. The mask was cleverly in place, as usual. 'Let me introduce my new secretary, Henrietta Melyn. Henrietta, meet Joelle Mercier, Marc's wife.'

Henrietta shook hands, murmuring a polite, *'Enchantée, madame.'* She fervently longed to escape, but there was nowhere to go. Nick was exchanging news with Joelle, who appeared to be a partner in Marc's agency, and therefore another business contact to impress with her efficiency. Good manners dictated that she kept a smile on her face, and a firm lid on her reactions to the discovery that the roving-eyed Marc Mercier was married, and that his wife Joelle appeared to be well-practised in the art of flirtation in her own right.

But don't make hasty judgements, she reminded herself quickly. Whenever she found herself tempted to jump to quick conclusions, she thought of her marriage to Tristan, and its nightmarish aftermath, and resolved to take a tolerant view. Things, as she well knew, were not always what they seemed . . .

But she found this noble sentiment hard to hang on to as the day progressed into evening, and, after a brief shower and change at Marc's remote stone farmhouse, they all went out to eat together. Joelle, all cleavage and thighs in a tiny black sheath dress, totally monopolised Nick, who looked grimly irresistible and slightly decadent in silver-grey cords and black sweatshirt, and

Henrietta found herself in the embarrassing position of being apparently paired off with Marc.

The situation made her withdraw into a defensive coolness, chiefly to hide her bewilderment. Did the Merciers genuinely have an 'open' marriage? Or was she just being naïve and easily shocked by sophisticates who played complex games?

Whichever way she looked at it, the friendly camaraderie of her earlier meeting with Marc now seemed weighted with too much sexual innuendo for Henrietta's taste. She kept her eyes on her plate as much as possible, and kept her spirits up with frank appreciation of the superb food, the exquisitely cooked red mullet in shrimp sauce, the aromatic French bread, the crisp lettuce tossed in olive oil tasting as it never tasted at home. Her steak was redolent of butter and garlic, and blended mouthwateringly with the tiny diced fried potatoes. Even the statutory *crème caramel* tasted creamier than usual.

'You seem deep in your thoughts, Henrietta.' Marc's dark eyes were smiling at her across the dinner table, and he reached across to take her hand. Recoiling as politely as she could, she quickly picked up her cup and sipped her coffee, too bitter and strong for her taste but redeemed with a dollop of cream, requested by Nick in a gesture which surprised her. While they'd eaten out together relatively recently, she was still astonished that he should remember how she liked her coffee.

'I'm afraid I'm tired,' she confessed, suddenly aware of Nick's attention. He appeared to be concentrating on another wittily amusing anecdote of Joelle's, all of which had so far seemed to amuse the story-teller more than the listener, but now she could feel his eyes on her.

'That was the kind of enormous meal which sends me straight to sleep!' she added apologetically.

'It is our French custom of eating so late.' Marc reached for the coffee-pot to replenish her cup. 'And we should perhaps not have brought you to our favourite *boîte* to eat? All this music is tiresome for you, so late at night?' The black eyes were teasing, and she laughed involuntarily.

'Heavens, you make me sound like a geriatric!'

'Not at all, Henrietta. You are at least ten years younger than anybody else at the table!'

'*C'est vrai*, Marc,' Joelle interrupted, an edge to her voice. Was it because she'd lost Nick's attention, or because she resented having her own age so unchivalrously highlighted? 'It must be way past Henrietta's bedtime— why don't you take her home to bed, *chéri*?'

The arch innuendo brought a flood of hot colour to Henrietta's face, and a sick feeling to her stomach. She felt like being exceedingly rude to Joelle Mercier, but her secretarial training came to her rescue. Discretion and diplomacy at all costs. But she was deeply grateful for the dim candlelight.

Nick stood up, unhurriedly, with a graceful flex of his muscles.

'I'm sure Henrietta will manage to keep her eyes open long enough to dance with me,' he murmured smoothly, grasping her arm before she had a chance to demur. 'And if anyone's taking her to bed, let me remind you that she's *my* secretary!'

This was added with such deadpan flippancy that both the Merciers laughed, and the brief moment of tension appeared to be defused.

Henrietta's tension was far from defused, however. Stiff and unyielding, she permitted Nick to steer her on to the tiny dance-floor, then glared incredulously at him as he drew her into his arms.

'Was that supposed to be a *joke*?' she exploded, rigid with anger. 'In my whole *life*, I haven't come across anyone as . . . as *arrogant* as you!'

Nick did a mock recoil, but his hold on her waist didn't loosen. The music was a French ballad, soulful and heart-wringing. The couples around them on the floor were dancing the classic 'slow', barely moving. She made a brief effort to free herself and was rewarded by a tight-ening of the arms encircling her, bringing her sugges-tively close to the full length of his muscular body. Heat invaded her from head to toe.

'Calm down, Henrietta.' His fingers slid sensuously over the smooth, silky material of the amber shirtwaist dress she'd changed into after the conference. 'The Merciers are harmless relics from the permissive age. What you seem to lack is a sense of proportion. Relax. I like this dress—it matches your eyes.'

'Relax? With *you*, and your *friends* the Merciers around? I'd sooner relax in a snake-pit!'

'You're not enjoying your business trip so far, then? I like the way you've done your hair tonight, by the way. It suits you in that topknot.' He lifted a hand to touch the loosely secured curls, his wide mouth twisting. 'Are all these stripy streaks natural, or out of a bottle?'

'Will you stop it?'

'Stop what? Complimenting my new secretary on her appearance? You seemed to be enjoying Marc's flattery earlier . . .' The caustic undertone belied the bland inton-ation. The combination of smooth mockery and buried hostility was unnerving.

'Will you just stop *taunting*?'

The unholy gleam remained in Nick's eyes, but he was obediently quiet. But as the silence stretched on he im-perceptibly closed the gap between them, and to her chagrin she felt her body reacting to his closeness. The treacherous heat mounted. The impact of her reaction was so intense, it almost swept her breath away. Her breasts seemed to swell and ache, where she was pressed against his chest, and her stomach developed a curious melting feeling where his arm pressed her supple back into a bow, moulding her intimately against his hips. A low, persistent beat in the music seemed to echo the drumming of her own pulses. Nick bent his face closer, the teasing light abruptly dying from his eyes.

'I think I made a serious miscalculation, employing you as my secretary,' he said, his voice deepening.

'I agree.' Why did she feel so stifled?

'You do? Before you even know why?'

Her cheeks were burning. She'd had enough of his double-edged remarks, enough of his insinuations.

'Yes! And I'll tell you why you miscalculated. You seem to think I'm easy bait for your amusement. You think you can judge me for what you imagine happened in the past. You think you can despise me and mock me, even—oh, I don't know—take advantage of me?' Her brown eyes were burning with passionate intensity, and he stared back at her, silently. 'Well, let me tell you something, the reason I wanted to change jobs was to escape from my so-called "reputation"! Ridiculous, isn't it? The twentieth century, and I'm having to live down a "scarlet woman" label, nearly four years after the event? And I still keep coming up against prejudiced bigots like you! If you imagine I want to work for someone who constantly harps on about the past, who seems to actively despise me, you must think I'm a masochist!'

Nick expelled his breath in a rueful whistle. 'Quite an impressive speech, Henrietta. When I said I miscalculated, I meant that employing you has been a bit like opening Pandora's Box——'

'You haven't technically *employed* me yet!'

'You signed and returned your contract, Henrietta,' he pointed out calmly.

'That doesn't stop me from tearing my copy neatly in two and posting it back to you the second we get back to England.'

'True. But you won't do that.'

'Won't I?' Her eyes were blazing up at him. 'After your insulting remarks about my reactions to Tristan's death, in front of Marc? Did you *honestly* think I'd just take that lying down?'

Nick's mouth was grim, but one corner turned down in bitter mockery. 'You do seem to bring out the worst in me, for some reason.'

'Oh, of course, it's even my fault that you can't keep a civil word in your head in my presence!' Her voice cracked slightly, but she held on to her composure with the greatest difficulty.

The glitter in the green eyes was somehow slightly menacing. She tried to draw out of his arms, but failed to make any impression on the steely grip around her.

'Can you deny you were actually living with Tristan's oldest friend, when Tristan fell into the Thames?'

'No, but——'

'Martin Harvey, wasn't it? The man who'd been best man at your register office wedding only a few months previously?'

'Have you made it your life's hobby, studying every move I've ever made?'

Again, there was a twisted smile, coldly lacking humour. 'That may be a slight exaggeration. But that was the aspect which Giles found hardest to take. The fact that you'd moved in with another man within a matter of months of marrying his younger brother.'

'Things aren't always as straightforward as they seem.'

'True. I'm sure they're not. I suppose you're going to say that sexual attraction is a strange, uncontrollable urge, and you simply couldn't help yourself?'

'No! It was nothing like that! It was nothing to do with sex!' Her outburst turned a few curious heads their way, and Nick's arms tightened slightly around her. His gaze was penetrating as he looked down at her agitated face.

'Well...if we're getting right down to true confessions, I admit I would like to know the whole story of your relationship with Tristan, Henrietta...'

The unguarded outburst was quickly regretted. She had herself under tight control again.

'The whole story? From the barbed remarks you've been making I got the impression you considered yourself an expert on the subject! I'm quite sure you feel there's nothing left to know,' she retorted, in a quieter voice, adding smoothly, 'So can I go and sit down now?'

'You don't like dancing with me?' His voice was low and mocking.

'To be honest, I consider it beyond the call of duty. I'm quite sure Joelle is panting to dance with you, whereas I'd rather be talking to Marc. At least he appears to know elementary good manners.'

'And he'd also like to add you to his long list of extra-marital affairs. This could be his lucky night—he's found himself a lady with plenty of experience in such matters!'

Lashing out with her hand wasn't a premeditated thing, it just came as a furious reaction to the goading words. Her palm connected with stinging accuracy, and her fingers tingled as she dropped her arm and stared at the darkening patch on Nick's cheek.

'You little bitch——' She didn't wait to hear what else he had to say to her, in that ominously soft voice; she pushed her way blindly off the dance-floor, snatched her bag from the table where Joelle and Marc were witnessing the whole thing with varying expressions on their faces, and made a bolt for the ladies' room.

A desperate look at herself in the mirrored walls confirmed the worst. She looked the way she felt, with a hunted look, like a fawn at bay, all legs and eyes. Her pupils seemed to have dilated enormously, making her wide-set eyes almost black instead of gold-brown. Rapidly smoothing her hair, she took a few deep breaths to compose herself. This was crazy—she'd never before in her life slapped a man across the face. It was one of those actions you saw only in B-movies, something she'd always thought impossibly far-fetched and unlikely.

She sat down for a few minutes on one of the velvet-topped stools, composing herself, trying to sort out her confused feelings. Nick Trevelyan was just so...provocative. It was as if he needed to constantly goad and taunt. Why, she hadn't a clue. Unless he was one of those males who had to keep proving his masculinity, in case any jumped-up female should dare to question it. Maybe he'd had a love-hate relationship with his mother, or something.

Smiling involuntarily at her amateur analysis, she stood up and splashed water on her face, and felt slightly better. The shivery heat had gone from her body, and she acknowledged that her feelings on the dance-floor hadn't been solely centred round indignation and hurt pride. The feel of his body moulded intimately against hers still lingered in her senses. The fact that she could have felt so physically overwhelmed by a man she deeply disliked was not something she felt like facing up to, right now...

'Are you going to hide in here all night, Henrietta? I've been sent to see if you are all right!'

Henrietta jumped involuntarily as Joelle Mercier's cat-like blue eyes appeared in the mirror behind her, malicious amusement only just veiled by a veneer of concern.

'I'm quite all right, thanks.'

Joelle gazed at her pityingly. 'You don't look all right, *chérie*. Take a word of advice—do not throw yourself at Neeck the way you did just now on the dance-floor...'

'*Throw* myself at him? What on earth are you——?'

'Hush, hush. So angry, so indignant!' Joelle's smile was infuriatingly supercilious, as she flicked back her heavy chestnut hair. 'Just remember he has too many females falling into his bed—too many young girls falling passionately in love with him! Neeck prefers the...safety...of more mature women, *chérie*!'

'Why? Because they don't slap his face quite so often?' Henrietta hazarded grimly, loathing the idea that the three of them had been sitting laughing about her open display of temper, and trying very hard to ignore the severe twist of pain caused by Joelle's apparent closeness to Nick. The anger part made sense, the pain didn't...

'Because they don't try to trap him, *ma pauvre petite*. And don't imagine that slapping his face proves you are not attracted to him, Henrietta—hate and love are very mixed up together, didn't you know that?'

'I think you're the one who is mixed up, Madame Mercier.' It was a supreme effort to speak levelly, to insert the necessary disdain into her voice. 'So save your advice for one of these females who are falling passionately in love with Nick Trevelyan—I assure you I'm not one of them!'

It took all her reserves of poise to walk past Joelle and back into the darkened nightclub, aware of the older woman's eyes boring into her back as she went.

Nick was leaning back in his chair silently, watching their return, smoking one of Marc's pungent Gauloises, something she hadn't seen him do before. As she approached, he abruptly suggested they leave, and the Merciers seemed happy to comply.

The drive back was a tense affair, for Henrietta at least. Whatever explanation Nick had given to the Merciers while she'd been in the cloakroom, nobody commented openly on the scene on the dance-floor, which made for a rather more charged atmosphere than normal. Joelle and Nick sat in the front, and Nick drove again, demonstrating to Henrietta yet another facet of his power complex. He had to be in control, she reflected darkly; he couldn't possibly sit back and let someone else drive him, even in *their* car! To keep her mind off Marc's unwelcome closeness, a few inches away from her on the back seat, his arm resting casually along behind her, she brooded with obscure satisfaction on this and numerous other character flaws as the men talked sporadically about the merger, and Joelle dozed, her sleek chestnut head resting on Nick's shoulder. An inexplicable streak of hot anger tore through Henrietta. If it hadn't been completely clear before, it was painfully clear now that Joelle was the 'safe', mature woman in question, she reflected wryly. And why that should cause this sick, dull ache in her chest, she was at a loss to understand.

It was a relief in more ways than one to arrive at the farmhouse, and bid hasty goodnights all round.

'I hope you have everything you need in your room, Henrietta,' Joelle purred, watching her as she carefully avoided Nick's eyes in the round of polite 'goodnights'. *'Dormez-bien.'*

'Thanks. And you.'

Henrietta had to stop herself running up the stairs to escape from those knowing, scornful blue eyes, and the square, high-ceilinged bedroom she'd briefly changed in earlier now seemed a blessedly familiar haven. Closing the door, she stared wearily round at the fresh yellow and white colour-scheme, and heavy dark oak furniture. Thankfully she had her own bathroom adjoining—she wouldn't have to risk bumping into either of the Merciers engaged in any nefarious night-games. And, even more important, she wouldn't risk bumping into Nick Trevelyan.

It was a sticky, humid night. Closing the shutters, she raised the sash window a fraction then took a rapid shower before collapsing, exhausted, into bed, where she tossed and turned, until she recognised it was too hot for the mint-green cotton nightdress and discarded it on to the floor beside her.

Still she couldn't sleep. Her brain was over-active. Replays of Joelle's scathing words at the nightclub, images of Joelle's head resting against Nick's broad shoulder as they drove home, kept swimming into her mind, all jumbled up with the feelings she'd experienced when Nick held her on the dance-floor, and that abrupt, violent episode when she'd lashed out at him. Rather belatedly, she recalled her brother Piers, and his high ambitions within Trevelyan Estates. Had she jeopardised her brother's career, through her own pride and temper? It did no good to assume that Nick Trevelyan was above such petty vindictiveness. He'd demonstrated a particularly nasty side to his nature so far, hadn't he?

The more she thought about that, the more she ached all over with a choked, confused misery which seemed to have no logic in it.

Finally, just when she thought the spinning images would drive her mad, she fell asleep.

It seemed only minutes later that she woke, thrashing and screaming, vaguely aware that she was tangled in her rumpled sheet and bathed in perspiration. Someone was restraining her, gripping her arms, shaking her a little. The remaining wisps of nightmare receded and she saw that Marc Mercier was sitting on the edge of her bed, a Paisley dressing-gown loosely belted round him, his face anxiously smiling and reassuring in the triangle of light from the open bedroom door.

'Henrietta, *calme-toi, calme-toi... Q'est-ce que c'est? C'était un cauchemar?* It was a nightmare?'

He sounded so avuncular and soothing, she felt silly tears spring to her eyes. Belatedly she realised the sheet was wrapped around her lower half but traitorously revealing her nakedness from the waist up, the generous swell of her breasts exposed, and she grappled with the material, beginning to tremble quite irrationally, when another, taller shape appeared in the doorway, and Nick's curt voice snapped, 'I heard screaming—what the hell's going on in here, Marc?'

Marc had jumped to his feet, and she took the opportunity to snatch at the bedclothes and cover herself.

'Nick—Henrietta was having a bad dream...' He sounded a touch defensive. 'I was coming up to bed very late, on my way up the stairs, and I heard a blood-curdling screaming...'

Nick, tautly muscular in a black silk dressing-gown, was ignoring him, staring at Henrietta, his heavy-lidded eyes unfathomable.

'I heard the screaming,' he said flatly. 'Are you all right, Henrietta?'

'Yes...yes. I'm all right now—sorry to disturb everyone...' She was trembling, she realised ruefully, half from the lingering horror of the dream, half from the present tension.

'You did not disturb me, *chérie*! I am a chronic insomniac! I was down in the salon, reading Nick's merger proposals. Unfortunately, they were too interesting to induce sleep!' The Frenchman laughed goodnaturedly, eyeing her recently exposed curves appreciatively now that they were under the thin sheet. 'But I am glad I was the first on the scene to offer assistance——'

'Go to bed, Marc.' Nick's tone was abrupt, the statement too harsh to make any pretence at civility.

After a short pause, Marc offered a mock salute, and backed obligingly out of the door, with a light-hearted *'bonne nuit'* as he vanished along the landing. Before Henrietta could protest, Nick came over to her bed and sat down where Marc had sat seconds earlier, leaning forward to flick on the bedside light and examining her with an unfathomable gaze.

'Do you always sleep with nothing on?'

'More data for my personnel record?' she parried tautly, clutching the sheet tighter and wishing she didn't feel so shaky and vulnerable after the bad dream. 'I don't know why you threw your weight about like that with Marc Mercier—unless you're so damned arrogant and *possessive* you think you're the only one entitled to enter your secretary's bedroom?'

'So I was interrupting something,' he mused harshly, raking her face contemptuously. 'I thought I might have been...'

'Oh, yes, you certainly were. Your untimely appearance quite ruined my nocturnal plans!' she agreed witheringly.

Nick stared at her for a long moment, then suddenly closed his eyes, raking a heavy hand through his already tousled dark hair.

'I'm sorry,' he managed to say through his teeth. 'Heaven knows I've no right to march in like this and criticise...' He stopped, rubbing his forehead wearily, glancing up at her with an imperceptibly altered expression in his eyes. 'What the hell was that nightmare about, Henrietta? You sounded as if you were being strangled!'

'It was just a nasty dream I sometimes have...'

'Do you want to tell me about it?'

She chewed her lip, suddenly conscious of the wild disarray of her hair, her nakedness beneath the sheet, of the threatening intimacy of this situation.

'I don't think I could, even if I wanted to. There's not enough logic in it. Lots of running away but not moving—and houses with something trying to get in at all the windows and doors and I'm running round trying to lock them all in time to stop whatever it is getting in...' She shrugged slightly. 'I can think of several more suitable occasions to have a heart-to-heart about my nightmares...'

He said nothing, considering her with an ominously patient expression on his face. Unnerved, she stared back. He looked immorally attractive, with a heavy five o'clock shadow on his strong jawline and sleep-shadows beneath his eyes.

'Would this nightmare of yours have anything to do with your marriage to Tristan, Henrietta?'

'Don't you ever have nightmares?' His uncanny accuracy threw her off guard, and she faked an enormous yawn to hide her sudden, acute agitation.

'Occasionally. I don't wake up screaming the house down, however.'

'Do you live alone?'

'Yes.'

'Well, then, you don't know if you scream and shout during your nightmares, do you?' she countered, pleased with her effort. 'And I could just as easily demand to know about your relationship with your brother Bevan!'

'What?' The stunned silence, followed by Nick's savage undertone, made her heart miss a beat.

'There are parallels, if you think about it,' she persisted doggedly. 'Both were people we were very close to, people we loved—and both of us were involved, either directly or indirectly, in their deaths...'

'That's probably the stupidest statement I've ever heard,' Nick stated finally, his voice dangerously even and controlled. 'My brother Bevan and I were involved in a car crash. He was killed, and I was injured, but survived. Your marriage to Tristan was a farce from the word go, according to Giles——'

'According to Giles! I suppose he's another flying fanatic, is he? You meet up regularly for looping the loop and chewing over the latest family gossip, do you?'

'Giles and I sail together. He's also my accountant.'

'Is he really? Well, he might be your accountant, and also Tristan's big brother, but he's not God, you know! He's not omniscient!'

'It was common knowledge you and Tristan lived a pretty wild existence up in London,' Nick went on remorselessly. 'The high life, parties——'

'You've never been to a party, I suppose?' Her taunt was defiantly flippant.

Nick shrugged slightly, unmoved. 'I've been to plenty of parties, but not the kind to make the headlines in the gossip columns the next day. The tabloids had a field day, and who can blame them? Cornish MP's son and vicar's rebellious daughter run away to marry, straight from school, against their families' wishes...MP's younger son and his beautiful, wilful teenage bride hit the London party scene like bright new comets in the firmament!'

Henrietta felt sick. How often had she tried to block that whole episode from her mind? Tonight, to have it resurrected and thrown in her face, like a handful of dirt, from someone who'd abruptly re-entered her life from even further back in her dim and distant past... She wasn't sure which was worse, the nightmare, or this...

'Don't you ever give up?' she demanded angrily. 'I'm tired of you poking your nose into my private life. I thought I made my feelings crystal-clear at the nightclub!'

A slight glint of amusement appeared in Nick's narrowed eyes. 'You mean by slapping my face?' He fingered his jaw gingerly, his mouth tilting downwards. 'At least I didn't hit you back.'

'I must say, that surprised me. I wouldn't have put you in the gentleman category.'

'I was always taught never to hit females...Henrietta...'

'Nick . . .' She caught her breath unsteadily, bracing herself. 'I feel I should apologise for hitting you like that! I . . . I hope I haven't . . . that is . . . I'd hate to think I'd jeopardised *Piers's* position in your firm in any way by——'

'Piers still has to justify his position in my firm, Henrietta,' he cut in softly, and she stared at him uncomprehendingly as his wide mouth twisted. 'Whatever happens to your brother I assure you it will bear no relation to your regrettably violent tendencies.'

The subtle switch from cool hostility to a gentler tone threw her into confusion for a moment. His comment about Piers had been disturbingly ambiguous. What had he meant by it? Wasn't he happy with Piers's work? This was so much at odds with the picture Piers painted of his relationship with Nick that she frowned in confusion.

'Piers has worked for you for about six years,' she pointed out. 'What are you talking about, *justifying* his position?'

'He's been with me for six years, but branch manager for only one of them.' He shrugged slightly, dismissively. 'The qualities I look for in a branch manager are slightly different from those I require in a good negotiator. I'm not saying Piers is not doing an adequate job. I am . . . reserving judgement for the present.' He raised an eyebrow at her mutinous expression, adding gently, 'Now, why don't you tell me about that nightmare?'

She rallied her defences with great difficulty, her anger storming back at his patronising reference to Piers.

'Frankly, you're the last person on earth I'd confide in. I might have told Marc, before you dismissed him like some subordinate employee! At least he was trying to be genuinely kind . . . I'd rather talk through my nightmares with him any night!'

'Would you?' Nick's tone was flat, hard to gauge. He stood up. 'In that case I'll get back to bed and leave the coast clear for him, shall I?'

'Oh, just go away, will you, please?' The slight crack in her voice made him lean to examine her face more closely, and she blinked away her tears fiercely.

'OK, I'll go away,' he agreed softly, a new glitter in his eyes as if he sensed her sudden vulnerability. 'But do you know what I'd really like to do right now?'

'I'm sure you're about to tell me!' Her throat was traitorously choked.

'I'd like to rip that demure little sheet away and accord myself the same dubious privilege Marc Mercier was enjoying when I came in just now!'

Her fingers clenched on the sheet, turning white with fury. The covert threat in his voice jolted memories. She was suddenly cold with irrational fear.

'Spare me the macho-man act!' she retorted, summoning all her courage to inject the right note of bored indifference into her voice. 'Joelle Mercier isn't around to watch this time!'

Nick was silent, gazing at her narrowly, his expression unreadable. Then he started to laugh, softly. His reaction brought a tinge of colour to her face.

'What's so funny?'

'I'm not sure,' he murmured, sobering slightly. 'Unless it's the impression that I've finally met a female as cynical as I am?'

'Just get out!'

'All right, I'm going...' He sounded slightly huskier, his eyes darkening on the contours of her body as she wriggled lower beneath the covers. 'But just before I go, there's something I need to prove to myself...'

And before she could evade him, he leaned down and kissed her, full and hard, on the lips.

She was too confounded to struggle. And in any case, the welter of sensations was a kind of exquisite agony. Abruptly, shockingly, her breath seemed to evaporate, and she lay motionless, her simmering anger melting away in a blur of tactile exploration. Dimly she registered a series of dislocated reactions; the coolness of his lips contrasting with the heat of his tongue as he probed hungrily between her lips, that subtle whiff of lemony musk aftershave, and above all the restrained but threatening power in his body.

With a hoarse exclamation, he slipped his hands behind her naked shoulders, drawing her up against him, and the sheet slid down so that her breasts came in direct contact with the roughness of his chest hair at the V of his dressing-gown. She made strangled noises in the back of her throat, beginning to tremble uncontrollably, and his arms tightened around her, crushing her to him with a surge of male possessiveness. His hands were warm and hard on her bare skin, stroking with a taut, restrained urgency.

'Henrietta... Oh, Henrietta...' The deep voice held a husky note she couldn't understand, but the hungry, devouring movements of his lips against her throat, burning a trail down towards her breasts, made his intentions only too frighteningly clear.

She did struggle then, but her movements seemed to ignite the heat between them and with a choked cry of panic she stopped, her senses stumbling between pleasure and fear. Nick Trevelyan's touch seemed to ignite her in a way no man's had ever done before, in a way which made her breasts tingle and her groin ache and burn as if some colossal electric shock were jolting through her.

The way he crushed her to him, possessive and confident and sensually aware of the shape of her body, was intoxicating and terrifying at the same time.

Then, with a rough, almost violent exclamation, he let her go, almost thrusting her away from him, and straightened up abruptly, gazing down at her bleakly, seeming to be struggling for breath.

'I'll let you get back to sleep now,' he murmured hoarsely, stepping back from her as if for his own protection as much as hers. 'And this time I'll wish you sweet dreams, Henrietta...'

She couldn't speak, and her only consolation lay in the realisation that Nick looked as dazed and shaken as she felt, as he let himself out by the bedroom door.

CHAPTER FIVE

HENRIETTA had overslept. They'd agreed on breakfast around nine, and it was five minutes past that already. Struggling out of the mists of sleep, she levered herself out of bed, took a hurried shower and, after a frenzied riffle through her overnight bag, opted for a calf-length yellow cotton skirt, button-fronted, with a low hip basque, and pulled on a loose yellow and white T-shirt to go with it.

Slipping bare feet into flat white shoes, and cinching her waist with a matching leather belt, she eyed her pale cheeks and tousled hair critically in the mirror. After a rapid attack with the hairbrush, her fingers trembling with impatience, she plaited her hair in a loose rope and secured the end with a yellow band. It would have to do, she decided, giving her appearance a despairing inspection before dashing downstairs.

Her late arrival made her feel at an immediate disadvantage as she joined the trio on the terrace.

Joelle's cool *'Bonjour. Tu as bien dormi?'* seemed a deliberate taunt, in view of the night's events. Had she slept well? Of course she hadn't slept well; she'd spent the most restless night of her life so far, her thoughts whirling round endlessly, with Nick Trevelyan's mocking face featuring in every vivid scenario. She glanced once at the *soignée* Frenchwoman, cool and elegant in crisp white linen suit and silky Hermès scarf knotted at the neck, then avoided glancing at her again.

'You are looking very charming this morning, Henrietta.' Marc was smiling at her. 'Come and sit here beside me—you prefer *chocolat chaud* to coffee, *c'est vrai*? I will call Anna to bring some for you.'

While Marc was waving towards the kitchen window to attract the attention of the young girl who came in to help them when they entertained, Nick lowered his coffee-cup and smiled humourlessly at Henrietta.

'Charming, I agree—positively schoolgirlish, in fact, with that plait. But a fraction heavy-eyed? Didn't you sleep too well, Henrietta?'

The long green eyes held an unreadable expression as he met her gaze across the table, and she stared back woodenly. If she showed signs of a sleepless night, she felt an unworthy stab of satisfaction to see faint shadows under Nick's eyes—did they denote an identical problem?

The smile in his eyes warmed, just a fraction, and a shiver of apprehension made her stomach contract. There was something different in Nick's attitude to her this morning. A knowledge? She shivered again, furious with herself and with him. Damn the man. If he imagined he only had to *kiss* her to cancel out all the veiled taunts and open insults so far this weekend, he was about to discover his mistake.

'I slept very well.' She smiled casually, helping herself to a hot croissant. 'But I must apologise for waking people up. My nightmares always seem much more dramatic than they really are.'

'Nightmares when you wake yourself up screaming must be pretty dramatic! Can you remember the details?' Joelle tossed her chestnut mane from her shoulders, fixing her with an analytical stare.

'No, I never can.' It was a glib lie, but Henrietta wasn't about to discuss her dreams over the breakfast table with

Joelle Mercier. The way she felt this morning, she'd be glad if she never had to meet the woman again for the rest of her life!

'What's the programme for today?' she asked Nick coolly. 'What time are you planning to fly back?'

'This evening. Marc's going to show us over some of their West Brittany offices, and if there's time we'll take a quick look at some properties likely to interest the British market.'

'It is a pity you couldn't stay longer,' Marc said, draining his coffee-cup. 'But I'll go through your proposals with my *notaire* and come over to Cornwall maybe middle of June? *D'accord*?'

'Agreed.' Nick was leaning back in his chair, stretching, the outline of his body hard and lean in beige cords and tan checked shirt. 'You and Joelle will both be more than welcome, of course.' He smiled at Joelle, adding smoothly, 'Are you coming with us this morning?'

'No. I've got an appointment. But I'll be coming to England soon, Neeck. And in England, you will have my *undivided* attention, *chéri*!' The low, intense voice, and the way she levelled a direct, challenging gaze at him, struck Henrietta as embarrassingly revealing.

She looked away quickly, unwilling to identify the stab of pain knifing through her. Had they slept together last night, under Marc's nose, before her unwitting diversion with the nightmare? It didn't bear thinking about. Helen *had* warned her, hadn't she? Naïvely she hadn't quite grasped what Nick's 'having a reputation' could entail. Now it appeared it meant a man who used women to suit his own purposes, regardless of moral rights and wrongs. Did Nick Trevelyan actually dislike women?

The legacy of that expert, skilful interlude before he left her room last night was a lingering, bewildering kind of excitement which infuriated her by its sheer persistence. Surely she couldn't find *this* man, of all men, physically attractive? That really would be the irony to end all ironies!

She finished her croissant, and sipped the delicious hot chocolate, her thoughts uncomfortable.

Their whistle-stop tour around a few of Mercier Immobiliers's offices took up most of the morning, and the remainder of the time was spent driving around the lush countryside to look at a selection of glorious Breton stone properties similar to Marc's. Converted barns, old mill houses, modernised village properties, tumble-down *fermettes*. Henrietta was enchanted by them all, particularly a glorious old stone manor, rambling, three-storeyed, swathed in wisteria, drowsing by a river in the spring sunshine.

'It's so beautiful around here. I'm amazed all these lovely houses aren't snapped up by the French themselves!'

'Many of my friends think I am quite mad,' Marc confided, chuckling. 'They prefer to live in town, and always if they can afford it to buy a place by the beach. To them, farmhouses are for farmers!'

'A big country house surrounded by lots of land,' Henrietta said thoughtfully. 'That's what most of the people I know dream of owning. I suppose that's why so many English people are interested in buying farmhouses in France? There seem to be so many *more* of them, and they're so much cheaper!'

'At the moment they are!' Marc laughed, and Nick glanced across from the driving seat, with a short nod of agreement.

'I'm tempted to buy that last one myself.'

'The manor at Pont-Ménel?'

'That's the one. What do you think, Marc?'

Marc nodded vigorously in approval. 'With the river frontage and the private jetty—a good buy, *mon ami*. It's not too far from the airfield, it has ten bedrooms, outbuildings, stables, ten hectares of land . . . Shall I put in an offer for you?'

Nick laughed grimly. 'I see you're catching on fast to the hard-sell approach, Marc, but don't waste it on me! I'll let you know when I'm ready—I've got enough on my plate in Cornwall at present.'

'*D'accord*—just let me know when you are ready— I've got dozens for you to choose from!'

The warm May sun shone steadily all day, and when they stopped at a *crêperie* for a quick lunch, Henrietta felt grateful for Marc's presence as a buffer between herself and Nick, so that she could begin to relax and enjoy just being in France again. Nick's company was impossible to relax in. There was too much unspoken tension, too many defences to put up. Now, by deliberately avoiding Nick's eyes, and concentrating solely on Marc's entertaining comments, she found she was absorbing familiar sights and smells, reliving happy memories of holidays with *Grandmère*, when she and Piers had run wild on the long golden beaches of the Ile d'Oleron, and sat in the harbour of La Rochelle watching the yachts come in.

'What about you, Henrietta?' Marc was asking, his dark eyes roaming appreciatively over her high, taut breasts beneath the yellow and white T-shirt. 'Why don't you buy somewhere over here yourself?'

She laughed. 'I'm not even a home-owner in England, Marc, let alone France! My earnings don't stretch to that luxury!'

'*C'est vrai*, Nick? You pay this talented, intelligent young woman such a pittance?' The joking question brought the prickle of heat to her neck, heralding a rare blush.

'Not at all, Marc.' Nick's retort was quiet, compelling her to look directly at him for the first time during their outing. 'When Henrietta gets her first salary cheque from me, she'll be able to negotiate a mortgage on a smart little house somewhere quite easily.'

'Will I really?' She injected bright insincerity into her voice, deliberately brushing the topic aside. Now wasn't the time or place to talk about her job as Nick's personal secretary, and whether or not she still intended to take up the offer. She was still seething inside at his treatment of her so far, but she had no wish to cause a scene in front of Marc.

'We'll see. I wouldn't want to commit myself to something I couldn't cope with.' The trace of ambiguity sufficed. Nick's jaw tightened, and she felt a twinge of unholy triumph. She tilted her glass to her lips and delicately sipped her *calvados*, relishing the sour apple flavour but wary of its potency. Just let him *try* to browbeat her into working for him, after his behaviour this weekend. He'd be sorry he ever tried. She should have known, right from the first moment of the interview, that it wasn't going to work. First thing in the morning, she'd start scanning the Situations Vacant again, and tell Nick Trevelyan to find himself another female to be nasty to.

* * *

The return flight was unnerving, the latter part completed in darkness.

'What happens if we accidentally bump into a British Airways flight from London to Paris?' she finally managed to query, nervously scanning the vast expanse of dark sky around them, and the inky-black English Channel far below.

'Hardly likely, since we're flying at a maximum of three thousand feet and they average nearly ten times that height, Henrietta. Plus, we're in constant radio contact with the various control points, and I'm a bloody good pilot...' His tone was hard to decipher. Light, possibly mocking, but with an underlying gravity which made her skin prickle.

He glanced at her, his dark face oddly cast in shadow by the dim red light from the gauges in front of them, and he put out a hand to lightly touch her knee.

'Henrietta...relax. You're in no danger. Watch out for the English coastline soon. You'll see the lights.'

'Please don't touch me.'

There was a taut silence, then a breathing space while Nick spoke via the radio and was formally handed over to another air space. Eventually, he turned to glance obliquely at her.

'Henrietta, I'm sorry.'

'Sorry?'

'I really screwed up, didn't I?'

She clenched her fists in the pockets of her light yellow linen jacket.

'If you're referring to using me for official target-practice all weekend, and parading me as an escape-route from your current mistress, yes, I agree.'

He let his breath out on a sharp, despairing sigh, and she stared woodenly out of the cockpit window at the approaching lights of the English coast, strung out like tiny fairy-lights adorning a model fairy landscape.

'Joelle Mercier isn't my mistress.'

'Well, if she isn't, she'd certainly like to be.' She gave a mirthless laugh, keeping a tight rein on her wavering emotions. Nick's intense mood was new, and she found it strangely moving.

'Joelle is a woman who likes men to notice her. She needs a lot of attention.'

'So do my twin sisters. Only they're ten years old and can get away with it.'

His sideways glance was wry. 'You sound almost . . . jealous?' he probed quietly.

'Don't be ridiculous!'

The radio crackled into fresh, frantic life, and the attempt at intimate conversation was abandoned. It wasn't until they were safely on terra firma, and driving homewards in the Alvis, that Nick resumed his offensive.

'We need to talk about last night.'

'Do we? Not content with verbally insulting me all weekend, you . . . you *attacked* me, forced yourself on me, just to . . . to prove something to yourself! Why should I want to talk about that?' She found she was shaking slightly from the prolonged tension of being in Nick's company.

'Because you're not being honest.'

'Not being *honest*?'

'When we kissed, Henrietta, you enjoyed it as much as I did!'

She could hardly breathe for a few seconds.

'You're going the wrong way,' she pointed out shakily, as Nick took the St Wenna turn instead of the main road into the centre of town. 'Would you mind dropping me off at Wharf Street?'

He shook his head abruptly. She glanced at him more closely, trying to decipher his expression behind the up-turned collar of his leather jacket. He looked bleakly preoccupied, his long eyes half lidded, as if he was mentally weighing up a problem.

'Neither of us have eaten this evening. We're going to my place. I'll cook bacon and eggs—one of my specialities.'

She stiffened for battle.

'Your place? No, thanks! I've got plenty of food in my own fridge, and I'm tired. You can drop me here, if you don't want to turn round. I can get the bus back.'

'No, we need to talk.' They were already driving up the long, hydrangea- and rhododendron-edged drive to Trevelyan House, a huge sprawling bulk of a house with the moonlight glinting palely on its rows of square-paned windows. She had to resist the improbable urge to fling herself out of the moving car and run for safety.

'We've nothing to talk about, as far as I'm concerned.'

'We need to talk about our boss-secretary relationship, which doesn't seem too healthy at present——'

'That's easily remedied. I'm not going to work for you!'

'And as for our personal relationship, Henrietta,' he continued implacably, sweeping the Alvis to a halt in front of a wide flight of granite steps, 'that leaves a lot to be desired as well.' He cut the engine and turned to look at her, and her heart gave a huge, anguished jolt at the sudden darkening of his eyes. 'Don't you agree?' he added softly, his mouth twisting into a grimace of self-mockery.

'Whose fault is that?'

Nick's expression grew darker. 'I think we both have a tendency to go on the attack, by way of defence.'

'Really? So what are we defending?'

'Ourselves?'

There was an uneasy silence. 'This is getting too deep for me, Nick. I'm tired and I'm miserable and I just want to go home.'

'And I'll take you home, just as soon as you've eaten some food and answered some questions.'

'Answer some questions? I should be the one *asking* the questions!' she burst out indignantly, and then to her chagrin saw his slight, triumphant grin.

'Precisely. I ask questions, you ask questions...that's what's known as talking, Henrietta. It's quite painless. Come on, let's go in.' His voice was deeper than normal, slightly husky.

With a vague sense of being outmanoeuvred, she climbed out of the car and followed him up the steps and into an enormous, book-lined entrance hall, where she stood staring around her idiotically, struck by the fact that she'd never been inside this house before, despite living less than a mile away nearly all her life.

'Cavernous, isn't it?' he murmured, watching her stunned inspection.

'I'd pity the estate agent called in to value it, that's for sure!' she said flippantly, her eyes hostile as she met his enigmatic gaze. She felt almost oppressed by the centuries of antiquity pressing in on her. The Trevelyans were rumoured to be rich. She knew, just as anyone else in this area knew, about property investments in Spain, about a virtual monopoly of the agricultural and country-house market, about a stranglehold on auctions, whether of houses or fine arts or antiques, but even so...

She stared round silently, taking in the priceless oil-paintings, hung above the bookshelves and framed in the wood panelling on the upper walls and the ceiling, the display cabinets full of flower- and bird-painted china which she suspected were Sèvres and Meissen and Worcester, then turned to Nick, with a slight shake of her head.

'No wonder you paled at the sight of my bedsit!'

'Ill-gotten gains of numerous long-dead Trevelyans. They dabbled in everything from copper to pilchards, with a spot of smuggling thrown in. Come on—finding your way around is rather like one of those children's adventure yarns...'

As he spoke, he pressed something on the wall and a concealed jib door in a section of the bookcases swung silently inwards, revealing the entrance to a vast sitting-room.

'I see what you mean. The twins would love this!'

'Bring them over some time. There's an attic full of old violins they could take their pick from, too.'

She glanced at him, her curiosity stirred in spite of her wary resentment. 'Have you lived here all your life?'

He shook his head. 'I've got a flat near the office, in Bodmin. I've only moved back in here since my father's death...while I supervise the alterations...'

'What are your plans for it?'

'I'm carving it into six apartments and selling the whole thing off—philistine, I know, but I'll renovate *tastefully*.' His glance was ironic, and her eyes widened involuntarily.

'Oh, what a shame! It's such a beautiful house...'

'I'm afraid it holds no sentimental memories for me. I'll be glad to be rid of it.'

His tone was harshly cynical, and she realised she was treading on delicate ground.

'What will you have to drink, Henrietta?'

'Um...I'm not sure. What goes best with bacon and eggs, I wonder?'

He caught the wry smile on her lips, his eyes glinting with a trace of amusement. 'We don't have to have bacon and eggs. I'm relatively adept at pasta, too. How about a glass of white Burgundy?'

'Sounds different. OK, fine. I'm sorry about your father.'

Nick's face twisted sardonically, and she felt herself stiffen in surprise.

'Don't weep too many tears for him.' He was un-corking a bottle and pouring out two glasses of wine, 'I think he'd had what he'd have described as a "good innings"!'

'How's your mother coping? She *is* still alive, isn't she?'

'Oh, yes, Mother's still alive.' He turned, his green eyes unfathomable again as he handed her the drink, but she detected a return of the defensive sarcasm. 'She's gone to stay with an aunt in Scotland while I sort every-thing out here, and produce a self-contained apartment she can come back to and manage by herself. But she's not too well. My father's death seems to have com-pletely thrown her.'

'Oh, I'm so sorry.'

'Here, try the wine.' Nick changed the subject smoothly. 'It's got an interesting bouquet, as the wine experts say!'

She took a sip, her mind still on Nick's parents. 'You seem...so bitter,' she said at last, watching the guarded expression in Nick's eyes.

'Do I?' He shrugged again. 'Maybe I am—it's not exactly intentional. There were undercurrents in my family. I always sensed I was the one being towed along by them!'

'Go on...'

'My parents had a relatively happy marriage, I think, but they had a nasty little habit of rowing about me a lot of the time.'

She made a wry face. There was a parallel there, in her own childhood, she reflected with a touch of surprise. 'What about?'

'My father wanted another ambitious trainee for the family firm. He couldn't understand why I couldn't be more like Bevan...'

'And your mother?'

'Mother was keen for me to pursue my musical inclinations. My father thought playing the violin was a totally unmasculine waste of time.' Nick's grin was dry. 'It led to periods of tension, to put it mildly. But I suppose they were reconciled often enough...those were my favourite times. When my parents were reconciled for a while, I got room to breathe!'

She absorbed this for a few moments, then frowned at him, perplexed. 'You mean your mother turned to you when she and your father were going through a bad patch?'

The wide mouth quirked in amusement. 'Only in the platonic sense, Henrietta. You're not uncovering anything incestuous.'

She bit her lip, more indignant than embarrassed. 'I didn't think I was! Where did Bevan fit into all this?'

'Bevan ranged himself with my father.'

'Because of the business, you mean? He was interested in the estate agency while you wanted to be a musician?

And your mother really wanted you to be a musician, so you were sort of allied with her?'

'In simplistic terms, I suppose so.' The defences were in place again, the shutters abruptly coming down.

She shook her head, with a faint, cynical smile. 'It was your idea, remember? Asking each other questions? *Talking*?'

Nick glared at her for a few seconds, then gave an abrupt, forced laugh. '*Touché*, Henrietta. OK, yes, my mother felt very strongly about my succeeding as a musician. She'd given up her own musical career, I suspect because she realised she'd never quite make the grade. So my talent was a vicarious sort of pleasure to her, I imagine.'

'So she must have been really upset after your accident...?'

He glanced at her with grim irony. 'Apart from the fact that her son Bevan had been killed, you mean?'

'I'm sorry, I didn't mean it to sound like that...'

'It's all right. I know you didn't.' Nick's voice was a touch gentler, and her heart contracted slightly. 'And, yes, of course she was upset. But, by then, she'd already given up trying to pull the strings, run my life. If there was one thing my earliest years taught me, Henrietta, it was to keep a healthy distance from possessive women!'

She was silent then, uncertain of precisely what he was telling her. His words sounded like some kind of gentle warning. But against what? Surely he couldn't imagine *she* had designs on running his life? Not even Nick Trevelyan could be *that* thick-skinned, could he?

'So you'll sell all this and then what? Buy that manor house in France? Commute?'

'Possibly.' He shrugged. 'The French way of life appeals. But I'm too much a Cornishman to let go of my links here completely. I'll aim for the best of both worlds, and see what happens.'

Nick had collected the wine bottle and was topping up their glasses, his smile wry.

'This is Puligny-Montrachet. Premier Cru. I decided to drink my way through the wine cellars as rapidly as possible to reduce the death duties.'

'That sounds like a recipe for disaster.'

'Don't worry, Henrietta. I have a strong streak of self-preservation. I've no intention of abusing my liver!' He smiled at her, moving slightly towards her and unsettling her composure so much she took an instinctive step backwards.

'Don't touch me, Nick, please…'

'Hey…' The deep voice was so gently quizzical, her heart seemed to turn over. 'Relax. I'm not going to forcibly seduce you.'

'I should damn well hope not!'

The silence hung, tense and laden with possibilities, between them.

'So what's it to be?' he said finally, breaking the growing atmosphere with a light, matter-of-fact tone. 'Bacon and eggs, or *spaghetti alla carbonara*?'

'Well, I do like *spaghetti carbonara*—but that's much more complicated than bacon and eggs…'

'Simplicity itself. Make yourself at home here for a while. I'll be back soon.'

It was hard to tell if she was being offered a genuine olive branch, or cunningly manipulated again. Alone in the enormous room, she wandered around uncertainly, almost unconsciously looking for signs of Nick Trevelyan's tastes as opposed to the stiffly conventional trappings of inherited wealth and privilege.

She finally tracked down a pile of professional magazines, some flying manuals, and a collection of compact discs, an eclectic assortment including classical orchestral, violin concertos, and some Celtic folk music. She felt tempted to slot one of the folk albums into the music centre concealed in a carved oak chest, but couldn't quite bring herself to do so. Make yourself at home, he'd said, but that entailed trusting someone enough to relax in their house. Trust definitely wasn't one of the feelings Nick Trevelyan aroused in her.

She was engrossed in a copy of *The Estate Agent* when he reappeared. Minus the leather jacket, in tight fawn cords and a fawn checked shirt with the sleeves rolled casually back, he looked disconcertingly attractive.

'Supper is served. Follow me.'

'Don't say we're eating in the baronial dining-hall, or something?'

'I'm afraid so. I've even lit the candles.' His grin was non-committal, but she felt her tension increase. Just what did Nick Trevelyan want from her? Was she to be a dogsbody employee he could vent his bitter sarcasm on whenever he chose, with the odd sexual fling thrown in?

She curbed her paranoid thoughts, and followed him calmly. Panicking at this stage would show him she was frightened of him, and she had no intention of giving him that satisfaction.

'This is very good,' she had to admit, when she'd taken her first few mouthfuls. 'Where did you learn to cook like this?'

'Self-taught. I enjoy it. I have a strange delight in collecting old cookery books.'

'You'll make a very versatile husband for someone, at least in the kitchen!'

She wasn't sure how she came to blurt that out, unless her third glass of the irresistible white Burgundy was to blame.

Nick eyed her thoughtfully. He took a sip of wine, the liquid glittering like molten gold as the candlelight reflected in the heavy lead crystal glass, his heavy-lidded gaze not leaving her face. She felt herself reddening, unable to halt the tell-tale colour warming her cheeks.

'Only in the kitchen?' It was a measured taunt, tinged with amusement.

'I'm quite sure you're versatile in every way!' she countered calmly, pre-empting his opportunity to take the tease any further. 'Have you never been tempted to marry?'

'Is this a proposition, Henrietta?'

'Don't be stupid!' The cutting retort flashed back like a reflex action, but she forced herself to laugh a little, her voice casual as she said, 'I just meant you're knocking on a bit to be still a bachelor.'

'I confess I hadn't seen it that way. Foolishly I'd been thinking I had a few years of life left in me, at just turned thirty! But let's say I've remained untempted by the whole stifling idea, Henrietta.'

She ignored the gleam of mockery in his eyes.

'Stifling? Why stifling? Most men look on marriage as a wonderful passport to freedom, don't they? Meals cooked, washing and ironing done, house cleaned, *and* sex every night thrown in with the deal. Can't be bad?'

'Is that how your marriage to Tristan was?'

She lowered her eyes from the sudden gleam of enquiry, and took another sip of wine, her heart beginning to beat faster. 'No.'

'So how did it differ?'

'What is this? Are you after the titillating details? Do you want to know whether we had sex every night, or whether I ironed his shirts?'

'I want to know why you married Tristan Melyn at all.'

She raised her eyes then, and met the pale, penetrating gaze as steadily as she could.

'Why do you want to know?'

'I want to understand.'

She stared at him dumbly, her throat drying suddenly. 'Tristan and I loved each other...'

'If that's the way you treat someone you love, lord help your enemies.'

She flushed crimson, putting her fork down with a clatter on her plate. 'You're a fine one to talk about *love*,' she shot back passionately. 'You don't know the first thing about it! You take what you want and then discard it!'

'Just like you did?'

'I didn't discard Tristan! I *had* to leave him! If I hadn't he'd have——' She stopped, choking against the tide of emotion threatening to overwhelm her. With a low, muttered obscenity, Nick stood up and came round the table, and pulled her gently to her feet.

'He'd have what, Henrietta? What would Tristan have done if you hadn't left him?'

'I think he might have killed me!' It was an agonised whisper, and to her chagrin the tears began to well up in her eyes, as if the relief of finally telling someone had unlocked the floodgates.

CHAPTER SIX

'IT'S OK, Henrietta, it's all right...' Could this deep, soothing voice be Nick's? Dimly, she registered that she was in his arms, held hard against his chest, and in danger of soaking the front of his shirt with her tears.

'It's all right now, let me go!' She wrenched herself free and turned away blindly to search out tissues in her bag. Fool, idiot, *idiot*, she cursed herself silently, scrubbing her face and blowing her nose violently, why tell *him*, of all people? She had friends, she had a close, protective, loving family, any one of whom would have offered a sympathetic shoulder to cry on. Why keep it bottled up for four years and then blurt it all out again to Nick Trevelyan?

'It's your fault,' she added, inconsequentially, turning a swollen face reluctantly back towards him. 'You've been topping up my wine glass without my noticing. I'm surprised the Gestapo bothered with torture—all they had to do was get their victims drunk and everything would have come spilling out!'

Nick smiled faintly, watching her with the penetrating intensity of a cat with its prey. 'Not everything, Henrietta. You haven't explained *why* Tristan Melyn could possibly have wanted to kill you?'

'I don't want to talk about it, Nick. I'd like to go home now.'

'Of course, putting myself in Tristan's shoes,' he began contemplatively, 'if my young bride happened to be

105

having an affair with my best man, I might well be driven to homicidal leanings...'

There was a sick feeling in her stomach, but she held his gaze steadily. 'I don't expect you to believe me. But I wasn't having an affair with Martin Harvey.'

'But you were thinking about having an affair with him?'

The innocent query was underlaid with a wealth of cynicism which warned her she was wasting her time. But she had a frightening sensation she'd unleashed a roller-coaster, just through letting that one sentence slip. She took a deep, shaky breath. 'Nick, when I said Tristan might have killed me, I didn't mean it to sound as if he was a raving psychopath! He just became prone to violent moods. He...he started hitting me. After the fourth time, when I had to spend a couple of nights in hospital, Martin suggested I have a spare room in his house—and that's all it ever was. A spare room in his house...'

She closed her eyes momentarily, the past vivid in her mind, the shame and the fear and the loneliness, the safe haven of that little mews house in Belgravia, Martin's kindness...

'Why didn't you go home?'

'And have everyone say "I told you so"? Besides, I was still hoping I could work something out with Tris. I might have been very young and silly, but I didn't enter into marriage *intending* it to end the way it did... I realise now I didn't really think things through...'

She saw his eyes flicker, and added bitterly, 'I don't expect you to believe me. But having blurted out part of it, I might as well tell you the rest for what it's worth. Tristan was my...my first real infatuation, I suppose...he always seemed so...carefree, so worldly wise...nobody told him what to do, he was the eternal rebel, and I got sort of caught up in his spell, I think... Oh, I don't know, maybe I wanted to make a statement of some sort? When my parents said, ''Don't see him any more,'' I just felt I wanted to dig in my heels and choose my own life! When Tris and I ran off to London, joined his favourite party set, and got married, I did it as much to show my independence as anything... Does any of this make sense to you?'

'Some—spoilt, headstrong youngest daughter defies her parents and plunges out into the big bad world? But none of it tells me why your marriage to Tristan ended up the way it did!'

She'd reddened slightly at his caustic words. 'I confess I might have been rather spoilt and wilful...but I wasn't the youngest daughter, remember—the twins came along when I was thirteen!'

'Mmm. And therein lies another story, no doubt.' Nick's tone was wryly amused as he observed her discomfort. 'And I sense you're not about to explain to me why things went so wrong between you and Tristan?'

'We just weren't...compatible...' She realised she'd been on the verge of confessing everything, and was appalled at herself. Nick Trevelyan was not about to become her closest confidant. Panic invaded her so abruptly, she felt a shiver of cold perspiration break out all over her. Looking wildly round for distractions, she spotted the cheese on the sideboard, with a glass bowl of dark red Californian grapes beside it.

'Is that dessert I see over there? Do you mind if I try a wedge of that cheese before I go?'

'If you like.' Nick moved quietly across the room and returned with cheese, fruit and small plates. 'It's Lanark Blue, Scottish cheese. I'll make some coffee. Help yourself while I'm gone.'

The cheese was creamy and blue-veined, but she ate it without tasting it properly, her emotions in a hopeless tangle. The need to escape and be alone to gather her defences had never felt greater, but Nick seemed intent on keeping her here and extracting confidences, and for some inexplicable reason he seemed to be succeeding. Was this his fatal charm? she wondered bleakly. An ability to prise out secrets, making a good show of listening with concerned interest?

'So you married Tristan thinking you knew him, and found you didn't?' Nick had produced a cafetière of strong dark coffee, and seemed intent on returning to the subject.

'Yes . . .'

'Do you want to talk about it?'

'Not any more.'

He passed her some cream for her coffee, and she poured it in a slow swirl of white against black.

'You don't want to talk about what turned Tristan from a carefree, party-loving rebel into a violent wife-basher?'

She took a swig of coffee, and stood up abruptly. 'No, I don't. What happened between Tris and me was private, nobody's business but ours. I'm really tired now, Nick. Will you take me home, or shall I call a taxi?'

'You could stay the night.' There was no expression in his voice, and no clue in his cool gaze as to what he was thinking as he watched for her response. Colour flamed into her cheeks.

'No, thanks.'

'In a spare room, of course.' Was there a deliberate tinge of irony in his use of the phrase? She picked up her bag, and glanced round for a telephone.

'Stop looking like a shocked virgin, Henrietta.' His smile was faintly mocking. 'I'm not suggesting we sleep together. I've no plans to start something with my new secretary. Helga will be back any minute, so if you're worried about being alone in the house with me...'

'Helga?' She couldn't keep the edge out of her voice, and was furious at the glitter of amusement it triggered.

'Helga was my parents' housekeeper.' He grinned calmly. 'My mother got her from an agency. I suppose I've temporarily inherited her.'

'How convenient for you.'

'Absolutely. I'm all for housekeepers like Helga. She has all the sterling qualities of a wife, without the inconvenience of the commitment. She certainly makes life extremely comfortable.'

He was deliberately goading again, and she should realise it by now, she chided herself.

'I see. I suppose Helga is six feet tall, blonde and blue-eyed, with a figure like Marilyn Monroe?'

'You've met her?' The laughter in his eyes should have been contagious, but she only felt like crying.

'Will you drive me home, please?'

'When I interviewed you I forgot to check on the most vital qualification of all,' Nick murmured, leading the way out to the car without further argument. 'A sense of humour!'

'Don't worry, I have one,' she managed to retort sharply, as she climbed into the Alvis and scented escape with a rush of relief. 'Otherwise I'd never have considered becoming your secretary in the first place!'

'Can I take that as your agreement to work for me, in spite of everything, Henrietta?'

'I'm not sure.'

'How about a month's trial? If you truly can't stand the sight of me at the end of a month, I'll write you a glowing reference and release you from all obligations. Agreed?'

She cast him a despairing glance, as they drove back towards Hone, and she couldn't keep the tug of a reluctant smile from her mouth as she met his eyes. 'Agreed. Though I suspect this is the worst decision I've ever made in my life, and with my track record so far, that is saying something!'

'Now that we know a bit more about each other, I foresee no problems whatsoever, Henrietta.'

She sat quite still as the car sped her homewards, thinking over his words, and wondering why she should feel so apprehensive inside at his glib, ambiguous prediction.

Outside her bedsit, she finally found the courage to put into words what was circling round in her head and making her feel dizzy with anxiety.

'There's one thing you said earlier—about...about my enjoying it, last night, when you kissed me?'

He twisted in his seat, and she felt a flush of heat creep into her face as he examined her expression in the shadowy street-light.

'Go on?'

'You were wrong. I didn't enjoy it...I'm not ready for any kind of sexual relationship with anyone, and I probably never will be.' The whole thing came out in a rush, and she bit her lip, clamping her hands into fists as his eyes slowly moved over her face. It was impossible to tell what he was thinking.

'So...when you shivered in my arms, and when you made those stifled little noises in your throat when I kissed you and touched you...you weren't enjoying it.'

'No!'

There was a prolonged pause. She felt almost paralysed, her legs too shaky to carry her weight.

'And you're telling me this just in case I was planning on including after-hours sex in the job specification?'

'Yes.'

'Henrietta . . . you don't need to be afraid of me,' he said at length, his voice calm and unfathomable, as he reached across and flicked open her door for her. 'I'm no sex-starved Lothario plotting to seduce unwilling secretarial staff, whatever you might think of me. The kiss last night just . . . happened. I respect your anxiety that I might be expecting something from you that you're not prepared to give. I'm willing to forget all about it, if you are. Agreed?'

She found her voice had deserted her, and merely nodded miserably.

'Fine. Any other conditions of working for me, Henrietta?'

She shook her head numbly, and began to climb out of the car.

'In that case, I'll look forward to receiving your report on the conference, and I'll see you in the office in three weeks' time. Goodnight, Henrietta.'

With an unreadable expression on his dark face, he stayed to watch her progress across the pavement and inside the front door of the house, before he drove away. And upstairs, in the privacy of her room, Henrietta threw herself down on her bed and sobbed and sobbed until she thought she'd never stop crying, until she felt so emotionally drained she'd never feel anything, ever again.

*   *   *

'Is the great lord and master there?'

The nasal voice on the telephone was oddly familiar, yet Henrietta couldn't be sure who it was.

'This is Mr Trevelyan's office...can I help you?'

'Is Nick in?'

'I'm sorry, Mr Trevelyan's away on business for a few days. May I ask who's calling?'

'I'm amazed you haven't guessed already!' Piers's laughing voice suddenly lost its nasal tone and reverted to normal. 'How's the first week going, Hett?'

'Oh, Piers! Do you have to be so childish?'

'Invariably. Besides, I don't call making phone calls holding my nose childish at all. Is he driving you like a slave?'

'I wouldn't say that. I like being busy.' Just as well, she reflected, glancing across her light, pastel-painted office to where Gillian sat frowning over the fax machine's latest offering. 'Gillian's here all week, showing me the ropes. So everything's going smoothly.'

'Good. Come and have lunch with me.'

'Lunch...oh, Piers, I can't...' Henrietta did a rapid mental survey of her stacked in-tray, her shorthand notebook half full of letters dictated before Nick left for Marbella yesterday, the list of telephone calls to make on his behalf.

'What do you mean, can't? You have to eat, don't you?'

'Yes, but I thought I'd grab a snack from the sandwich bar round the corner. I'm really very busy, Piers!'

'Too busy to call at the vicarage to see the parents, or ring Helen and Hugo, I gather!' Piers's light drawl set warning bells jangling in the back of her mind. The family had clearly noticed her absence and decided to make further enquiries. She sighed.

'I've had a lot to do. Changing jobs is quite a hectic time. We can't all slope off whenever we feel like it, paying social calls, living the high-life, impressing our latest *escorts*!'

'The art of delegation is a rare talent in a manager.' Piers calmly ignored her teasing barb about his penchant for lavish spending and his ever-changing parade of glamorous girls only too willing to help him with it. 'Seriously, Hett, remember that little fisherman's cottage you used to love, down at Port Quen?'

'The one built into the cliff?'

'I've just booked it on. The owner's emigrating to Australia to live with her daughter. It occurred to me you just might be interested?'

'I couldn't afford to buy anywhere...'

'Come on, Hetti! The great white chief's personal secretary always earns a packet. And according to Helen, you told her——'

'All right, all right,' she cut in hastily, before she could grow seriously annoyed, 'I'll come and have a look at it.' Didn't they ever give up? Organising her life between them? As always, the brief flare of rebellion left her feeling ungrateful and churlish. She'd needed them all, when Tris died...it wasn't very fair to resent their continued interest and concern, was it?

'Great, when?'

'Not lunchtime. This evening?'

'Done. I'll pick you up at seven.'

It was impossible to repress the faint surge of excitement at the thought of seeing inside the cottage she'd often longed to own. The prospect lifted her spirits and she sailed through the rest of the day, eating her sandwich and coffee with Gillian, and storing up the assorted snippets of information about her new boss with mixed feelings.

'His bark's generally worse than his bite,' Gillian confided cheerfully, proudly inspecting the shiny gold of her new wedding-ring. 'To tell you the absolute truth, I had a crush on him for years, before I realised I was wasting my time!'

'Wasting your time?' Henrietta raised her eyebrows teasingly, ignoring the sudden jolt of reaction in her stomach. 'Don't tell me Mr Trevelyan's not interested in women?'

'Oh, he's *interested* in them, but I think it's a question of safety in numbers!'

'Oh. Yes, I see.' She did see. Almost. Why did her stomach feel so churned up with misery? Because this sounded uncomfortably like a replay of Joelle's bitchy warning?

'Honestly, I worked for him for seven years! I reckon I know him pretty well.' Gillian tossed back her dark hair, clearly enjoying the superiority of long service. 'He was going to marry a girl called Annette Hexham—a stunning red-head, apparently. Then she went off with his brother. But when his brother was killed, in a terrible car crash, she wanted Nick back again.' Gillian waited triumphantly for a suitable response from Henrietta, and failing any went on, 'Nick was really bitter about the whole thing. He wouldn't have anything more to do with her. She rang him at the office nearly every day for about a month, and when he wouldn't speak to her she used to rant on to me about it... That's about the time Nick took up flying. I always say he did that to get away from Annette...'

Or from his mother? Henrietta found herself wondering idly, as she listened to the other girl's gossip without comment.

'I mean, you can't pester someone when they're a couple of miles up in the air, can you?' Gillian laughed at her own joke, then suddenly seemed aware that she was being decidedly indiscreet, and added apologetically, 'I've never told anyone else in the office all this, of course! It's just that you're his new secretary—it's best to know where you stand right from the start, isn't it?'

'Where I stand? I'm not sure I know what you mean...'

'You seemed very "chummy" together on Monday morning, that's all,' Gillian explained airily, dropping her paper cup and sandwich wrapper into the bin, 'It wasn't like Nick to relax and smile so much, but he's terribly moody. It wouldn't pay to get the wrong idea. Most of the females at Trevelyan Estates are hopelessly in love with him, you know. He's that kind of guy— must be his colouring, the dark hair and those cold green eyes! I'm just offering a friendly warning. Save yourself a lot of heartache and find yourself someone nice and reliable, like my Phillip.'

'Yes, of course,' Henrietta murmured politely, controlling herself with great difficulty. 'Don't worry, I *had* heard about Mr Trevelyan's reputation with women. Forewarned is forearmed.'

The telephone rang, and she gladly turned to answer it, avoiding Gillian's curious blue eyes. She'd wondered how Gillian put up with Nick for all those years, but now she found herself wondering how on earth Nick had put up with Gillian!

* * *

By the time Piers's brand new white BMW arrived outside her bedsit, twenty minutes late as usual, she'd swapped her smart black business suit for jeans and yellow sweatshirt, and eaten a scratch supper of beans on toast. Feeling a lot more human, she climbed into the car and beamed at her brother in anticipation. 'Have you got the details printed yet?'

'Not full details—here, I had this typed out for you today with all the information.'

She studied it as they drove, for once ignoring the beauty of the narrow lanes, barely noticing the creamy cow-parsley and froths of white blossom, the dog-roses and honeysuckle.

'It seems a very reasonable asking-price!'

'The old lady is in a hurry to sell,' Piers explained casually. 'She's keen to get to Australia to live with her daughter and grandchildren. I took Amy away for a couple of nights in a super country hotel up in the Cotswolds last weekend, by the way...had a fantastic time, good food, wonderful wines...'

'Lovely. I'm amazed you find the time, though.'

'Business was quiet. All work and no play, as they say!'

Henrietta recalled Nick's veiled comments about Piers, in Brittany, and glanced at her brother worriedly.

'Are you sure you're entitled to take all this time off, Piers? The offices are all officially open on Saturdays and Sundays, aren't they?'

'Like I said, a good manager delegates, didn't you know that? Life's too short to have your nose to the grindstone every minute of every day. You should indulge yourself a bit more, Hett. Get out more, build up your social life again...'

'I've got all the social life I want, thanks. I go swimming twice a week with a couple of friends, I go down to the tennis club sometimes...' She'd had enough of the wild party set in London to last her a lifetime. She preferred a quiet life.

'How about the folk club?' Piers asked suddenly. 'Do you still go and sing there?'

She shrugged. 'Occasionally. Not often.'

'Why not? You've got one of the purest voices around!'

'Too many memories.' She spoke quietly, not inviting further comment.

'Time you wiped out the memories, Hett.' Piers sounded unusually serious as he drew up outside Roscarrock Cottage. 'You can't live in the past, love.'

'Can't I?' She smiled at him obliquely, as they climbed out of the car. 'I sometimes wonder if I have much option! And I doubt if a quick rendering of my party-piece "Cam ye o'er frae France" would put everything right for me! Don't worry, Piers! I'm fine, really I am!'

Roscarrock Cottage was tiny two-up two-down, hewn into the rocky cliff at the end of a row of similar fishermen's cottages, nearest the tiny shingled inlet, where the Atlantic crashed in relentlessly in the winter months.

'I've always had romantic notions about this little creek,' she told Piers, as she gazed out of the upstairs window at the now peaceful water below. 'I think of all those wicked smugglers who sailed in here at dead of night, with their treasures from France!'

'Until they all got caught by the Customs man.'

'I wonder if they used this very cottage to hide their contraband?'

'I'll ask the vendor when I speak to her. What do you think, Hett? Do you want it?'

'I'd absolutely adore it.'

'You wouldn't be too lonely, stuck up here?'

She shook her head, following Piers down the tiny steep staircase and waiting while he locked up.

'Then trot off to the building society tomorrow, Henrietta, and I'll put your offer to Mrs Chivell without delay.'

'Thanks, Piers.' She gave her brother an impulsive hug as they stood on the rocky quayside.

'Consider yourself lucky to have an estate agent for a brother!'

Estate agency filled her every waking thought over the next week. Her firm offer to buy Roscarrock Cottage, subject to a surveyor's report, was overwhelmed by the volume of work at Trevelyan Estates. With Nick in Spain, and Gillian phasing out her visits to the office, Henrietta was faced with queries on the French merger, from Mercier Immobiliers, and at the same time bombarded with enquiries from the public about their French property service, following advertisements in the national newspapers. Unsure which of the other directors to turn to about Nick's European projects, she sent numerous frenzied fax messages to Nick in Marbella, but failing to get answers in time took a certain satisfaction in making various decisions on her boss's behalf.

'You've been busy, I see,' Nick commented, arriving unexpectedly at the office on the Friday morning, and scanning the folder of messages she'd laid neatly on his desk. She hovered at his elbow, keen to explain her actions.

'I took the liberty of phoning Marc Mercier about the various points raised by potential French investors—lots of people wanted to know about the legal processes involved, and the difference between the French and English systems. I drafted a summary—it covers local *notaires*, the *Cadastre* Land Registry offices, the *Société de Crédit Immobilier, Contrat de Vente, Signature de Pacte* . . . things like that . . . what do you think?'

Nick was reading through in silence, and she bit her lip, suddenly terrified she'd exceeded her duties. Finally he glanced up at her, his pale eyes more brilliant than ever against his freshly tanned complexion.

'Have you sent these out to people already?'

'No . . . I thought I'd await your authorisation. But I've discussed the same points on the telephone with people . . .'

'All this summary needs is details of the inspection flights we can offer—I've just done the deal on the new twin-engine six-seater. But well done. You've done a brilliant job, Henrietta.'

Her glow of pleasure was out of all proportion to the compliment. 'So if you give me the details of the flights, I can get copies of this printed?'

'By all means. I needn't have sprinted back from Marbella so fast. You've got the whole situation under control.'

'Thanks.' She turned away, unwilling to let him see her flushed face, but he reached out and caught her arm, twisting her back, his expression quizzical.

'You said you were ambitious,' he murmured, his eyes crinkling in the heart-stopping smile he'd wielded recently. 'I'm beginning to see why. Your executive abilities are outstanding.'

'Flattery will get you everywhere!' She laughed, wishing her heart would stop its tell-tale thumping against her ribs.

'Really? Would it get me a date for dinner tonight?'

'I'm tied up tonight,' she said awkwardly, conscious of his gaze on the V neck of her soft wrap-over silk blouse beneath the tailored jacket of her black gaberdine suit.

'That's a pity. I was planning on taking you for a quick test flight in the new company aircraft, and catching up on a few business matters at the same time.'

She hesitated. 'I'm going to a cheese and wine party at the vicarage, that's all. Why don't you come along? I'm sure we could legitimately talk shop in a corner.'

He raised an eyebrow. 'Gatecrash another family affair?'

'You'd hardly be gatecrashing as *my* guest! It's only one of my parents' musical soirées. Father masterminds them every few months to keep up morale in the church choir.'

His eyes were thoughtful, as he appeared to briefly consider the invitation. Then he nodded slowly. 'All right. Shall I pick you up?'

'If you like. I said I'd get there around eight.'

'Then I'll collect you at seven. We can have a drink on the way.'

She had to keep an icy grip on her wayward emotions for the rest of the day. It wasn't sensible, or logical, or intelligent to be feeling this idiotic glow of anticipation at the prospect of a couple of hours' socialising with her new boss.

But her traitorous heart still pounded faster when he smiled at her that evening, over the rim of his whisky glass in the cosily beamed bar of the Howel Arms at St Wenna.

'Here's to success in France,' he murmured, as she sipped her gin and tonic. 'And here's to my new secretary, who I freely admit I don't deserve.'

'I'm enjoying my new job immensely,' she assured him calmly. 'So let's leave it at that.'

'Suits me. You look very lovely tonight, Henrietta.' Nick's heavy-lidded green eyes roamed enigmatically over her loosely done hair and drop-waisted summer dress in a mauve and white flower print, making her skin tingle in the process. 'That floaty dress makes you look like one of Thomas Hardy's heroines. Very nymph-like.'

She took a steadying gulp of gin, and smiled brightly, keeping the images of Annette, Joelle Mercier and the mysterious Helga firmly in mind to quell the unsettling effect he had on her pulse-rate.

'Thanks. Shall we brave my parents' musical soirée?'

'This sounds slightly ominous!' He grinned, as they both stood up. 'But I'm ready when you are.'

'It shouldn't be too bad. But I confess it does help to be extrovert. There *is* a danger of being cornered and forced to do a musical turn!'

'In that case we'll definitely hide in a corner and talk shop!'

The vicarage was humming with conversation when they arrived.

'Lovely to see you again, Nick!' Mrs Beauman beamed, handing round drinks on a tray, and reserving a knowingly eloquent look for Henrietta at her surprise choice of partner. 'People are spilling over outside, so the crush isn't too bad! Thank goodness for another warm summer evening!'

Strains of a Brahms piano concerto being played with slightly rusty skill wafted from the direction of the sitting-room.

'That'll be Piers,' she told Nick, sipping her white wine and making a mental note to watch her alcohol intake. 'Brahms is one of his favourites.'

'Your brother Piers is a man of many talents,' Nick murmured, his face inscrutable, and she glanced at him quickly, wondering whether the comment was as straightforward as it sounded. She'd soon realised that, despite Piers's version of the relationship, there appeared to be little love lost between her brother and Nick Trevelyan. Piers's office wasn't making as much profit as the others, and whenever one of Piers's weekends away cropped up in conversation she'd detected a distinctly sardonic reaction.

'Well, it's perfectly possible to be an estate agent *and* be musically gifted. You should know!' Her light teasing failed to produce the desired response.

'If you're referring to my violin playing, I wouldn't know. "Gifted" isn't a word I'd apply to myself. Any ability I once had on the violin was the result of a hard, reluctant slog to please a certain member of my family!' The grim self-mockery was back. She gave him a startled look.

'Are you telling me you took your musical career as far as you did to please your *mother*?' she murmured incredulously.

'It wasn't a conscious thing at the time.' Nick took a swift mouthful of red wine, and smiled thinly. 'Just something I recognised in retrospect.'

'So you're saying the accident, being forced to give it all up... it didn't really matter?'

He shrugged slightly, taking two more drinks for them from a passing tray, and handing her the white wine. 'Not as much as everyone seems to think. As an object of local sympathy, I'm a bit of a fraud, really. I'm quite happy doing the job I do. I think I'm pretty good at it. I find it quite satisfying.'

'So why don't you play the violin more often?' she queried, frowning. 'I assumed you never played because you felt bitter and twisted about everything.'

'I don't play much because firstly it hurts my hand to play for any length of time, and secondly...' he breathed out abruptly, eyeing her with a strange air of surprise '...it has associations, I suppose. It brings back all those fraught years struggling to escape the apron-strings! What is this, Henrietta? Psychotherapy?'

'Of course not...'

'You know, it occurs to me that my normal interrogation skills fail miserably whenever I'm with you. I end up making all kinds of unwise confessions, and I get a blank wall from you in return. That's not very fair, is it Henrietta?'

'A blank wall?' She returned his look uncertainly, aware that they were cocooned suddenly in their own intense conversation among the swirling throng of guests. 'Bearing in mind all the highly personal information you prised out of me the night we got back from France, I really don't know what you mean...'

'Yes, you do. So far I've opened up under close questioning, which isn't something I make a habit of, and I still know very little about the real Henrietta Beauman. True or false?'

'Beauman?' She felt oddly vulnerable, suddenly, as if Nick was managing to pierce her mind and read all kinds of things she preferred not to think about. 'I'm Henrietta Melyn, remember?'

'Oh, I remember. But you'd prefer to forget, wouldn't you?' His voice was deeper, curiously gentle, and she felt tears welling perilously near the surface. She gulped some wine, appalled at herself, blinking rapidly and looking blindly round for an escape route.

'Nick, please...not now...'

'OK, not now. But soon. You need to talk about it. And lord knows, I want to hear it, Hetti...'

Their eyes locked and held for a breathless few moments, and then with a perceptiveness she hadn't credited him with, Nick took her hand firmly in his, and propelled her through the crush towards the cooler evening air outside.

'Isn't that a Flanders and Swan number I can hear out on the terrace?' He was steering her lightly through the French doors, where two of the St Wenna choir baritones were doing a hilarious double act. Guests were circulating casually between one 'impromptu' act and the next, giving the whole gathering a relaxed, easy atmosphere. But the contact of Nick's hand in hers made her far from relaxed. It was like an unspoken communication, an intimate hot-line of thoughts and feelings.

They joined the throng, greeting people and accepting another drink in due course from the circling trays, and when Nick released her hand she was conscious of an empty, almost unbearable sense of loss.

He seemed to know a lot of people. Moving around and chatting, they soon became separated. Piers had emerged from his piano recital and was holding court to a group of friends, with Amy, his latest girlfriend, a glossy model with scarlet nails and peroxided hair.

'Mrs Chivell's ready to move out within the next few weeks,' Piers assured Henrietta, grinning cheerfully. 'The place will be empty by mid-July. If you can get that mortgage sorted out, Roscarrock Cottage will be all yours before you know it!'

'Roscarrock Cottage?' Nick had joined them, interrupting his conversation with Helen's husband Hugo to frown enquiringly. 'Are you buying that, Henrietta?'

'Yes. It came on the market while you were in France...'

'That's strange. I saw Mrs Chivell in Bodmin earlier this evening. She didn't say you were her purchaser.'

Henrietta shrugged. 'She's been dealing with Piers. Why should she go into details with you?'

'Why, indeed?' His voice was cool. He seemed back to his enigmatic mood, and she was glancing curiously at him when the twins came running up, their blonde hair caught up in identical ponytails, tied with bright blue ribbon.

'We're playing the violin in a minute!' Juliette announced proudly. 'Daddy says we've got to! I bet you can't play as well as we can!'

Henrietta met Nick's eyes, and smothered a smile.

'I can't play the violin at all, but Mr Trevelyan used to play the violin very well.'

'Did you really? Can you play with us?'

Nick was silent for a moment, his expression deadpan. Henrietta held her breath. Should she have mentioned his violin playing? Or had the gin and tonic and the wine loosened her tongue too much?

'It depends how good you are,' he told them solemnly. 'It's a long time since I've played. You might show me up.'

'Oh, we're not very good,' Genevieve assured him earnestly. 'We haven't been learning very long. Can you play "Twinkle Twinkle Little Star"?'

'I should think I could manage that.'

Whoops of delight greeted this. Slightly nonplussed, Henrietta joined Helen and Hugo a few minutes later and stood in an appreciative crowd while 'Twinkle Twinkle Little Star' was given a memorable rendering by a tall dark man, in olive cords, white shirt and suede waistcoat, flanked by two very small ten-year-olds, on the sloping lawn of the vicarage gardens.

'Play something else, Nick.' It was Piers who suggested it, sauntering over with a drink in his hand, his eyes lighting up at the scene before him. 'How about a quick rendition of "Dancing Under The Rose" for old times' sake? Hetti will sing it. She knows it like the back of her hand, don't you Hett?'

She shot an outraged glance at her brother, but, short of throwing a girlish fit of shyness, she saw little option but to brazen it out. Pulse-rate leaping off the scale, she went to stand beside Nick in the circle of grass in front of the old sundial, and in the red glow of the setting sun she sang the haunting, evocative words of the old folk song, the strange poignancy of the situation lending an extra degree of purity to her voice, and an almost sixth sense of timing and anticipation of Nick's breath-taking fiddle performance.

The brief silence following was suddenly broken by a spontaneous outburst of clapping, and calls for more. But Nick had ruefully dropped the violin at his side, and she noticed how he surreptitiously flexed his left hand after the unfamiliar strain of holding the instrument.

'Sorry to disappoint our fans!' He grinned, handing the violin to Henrietta's father and grabbing Henrietta's arm to lead her inside, ducking the sudden limelight among the milling guests in the sitting-room.

'You might have warned me we'd be singing for our supper!' His voice was taut, amusement tinged with something else she couldn't quite decipher. 'That's an amazingly difficult piece to sing, Hetti. You were incredible!'

'You obviously haven't forgotten how to play the fiddle, either! You were brilliant!' She laughed back, her eyes locking with his and her heart almost tumbling into her mouth at the surge of elation she felt. The stimulus of the shared performance seemed to have broken down some unspoken barrier. An electric tension seemed to crackle between them, and the way Nick's eyes darkened as he gazed at the fullness of her parted lips showed that he felt it too. Her heart began to hammer.

'Let's get out of here!' he muttered roughly, grabbing her and propelling her into the hall. 'I need to find somewhere we can be alone!'

CHAPTER SEVEN

'NICK, for heaven's sake, everyone's staring...'

'To hell with them.' He looked and sounded grimly determined as he marched Henrietta towards the car and thrust her none too gently into the passenger-seat. 'I've been going slowly insane ever since that weekend in France...and tonight, right or wrong, there's something I have to find out...'

'Nick, where are we going?' She'd intended this to be a blunt demand, but instead her voice came out faint and unsteady. The subtle magic of that moment when their eyes had locked, after their shared performance, seemed to have affected her ability to think rationally. Her heart was drumming madly. Tension had crept into every part of her body, and Nick's rapid negotiation of the hairpin bends and steep descents towards Port Quen served only to increase the build-up of apprehension and anxiety. When he finally braked to an abrupt halt at the end of the narrow one-track road leading to the rocky cove, she was trembling all over.

'Let's walk.' Nick's suggestion brooked no argument. Climbing out of the car, she followed him along the dark, pebbly track towards the pale glint of washed sand. The sea was on its way out. The beach was hard and wet under their feet, only a tiny crescent of dry sand remaining under the towering cliffs.

Taking her arm, Nick steered her towards the cliffs, choosing a broad flat rock as a seat. She stared around her in growing panic. The sun was setting, late, just behind the jut of the headland. The brooding hogsback cliffs were turning pink and gold and violet.

'Why have we come here?' She whispered it as he turned impatiently to scan her face, the almost palpable fear he encountered producing an abrupt, unrepeatable obscenity under his breath.

'Hetti . . . for pity's sake, don't look at me like that . . .' His voice had a rough tenderness which jerked a buried nerve deep inside her, and she felt her throat fill with unshed tears, appalled at the intensity of feeling he appeared to be able to provoke in her. 'I don't know what happened between you and Tristan, Hetti, because you won't tell me . . . but I vow to you I'm not the type to resort to violence to get my own way . . .'

He reached out to cup the pale oval of her face in his hands, examining the tense, defensive set of her soft mouth, running a light finger over the full curve of her lips.

'You can trust me, Hetti,' he went on, his voice uneven, hoarse with emotion she didn't understand, was too keyed up to decipher. 'I won't hurt you . . . but these conflicting signals are driving me wild . . .'

'No, Nick, please . . .'

'Just let me kiss you . . .' he breathed shakily against her lips, and then covered her mouth with his own, pulling her harder against him.

The touch of his mouth on hers, the demanding probe of his tongue between her lips, the warmth of his subtle, expert invasion of the inner recesses of her mouth, triggered a quivering, tentative hunger within her. The past lost focus, blurred into unimportance. Now was all that counted, here, now, this tantalising ascent into excitement . . .

'I had to kiss you again...' he murmured huskily against her lips, long fingers caressing her slender back, skilful and soothing, slipping higher to caress the tender nape of her neck and to grasp the back of her head. 'I had to reassure myself I wasn't hallucinating last time...'

'Oh, Nick...this is all wrong...I can't...it's no good...' She wasn't making sense, she knew it, but the sensations flowing through her from head to toe were like a drug, sapping intellect, enveloping her in a glorious swelling anticipation which was a totally new experience, and for the first time she allowed her own fingers to stroke tentatively over his shoulders, then with a low cry slid her hands around his neck and touched the crisp spring of his dark hair, shivering as his arms tightened convulsively around her.

'I can't believe the way you make me feel...' The deep whisper of desire brought a flush of heat all over her body, and then somehow she was down on the sand, with the cool granular texture beneath her bare legs as the floaty hem of her dress blew up in the breeze off the sea. No, not the breeze, it was the long, intoxicating caress of Nick's hands as he stroked the soft contours of her thighs, running his fingers up over the silken plane of her stomach to her swelling, throbbing breasts, murmuring thick, hoarse words in his throat as he flicked open the zip of her dress and drew the gauzy material down.

'Hetti...*Hetti*...!'

'Nick, I don't...I'm not...' Rational thought vanished as she convulsed helplessly beneath the erotic joy of his mouth as he bent to suckle each hot, aching nipple, the lean hardness of his hands revealing a surprising shakiness as he cupped the soft mounds of her breasts in his fingers, and she heard herself cry out, soft, choking sounds in her throat as the tremors of passion shafted, unbearably sweet, down through her stomach and groin. She was trembling too, now, almost weeping with the power of emotion, dimly aware of the danger of the swift current of desire flowing between them yet too paralysed to stop it.

'You're so beautiful, Hetti, I want you so much...' Nick, too, sounded as though he were drugged, out of control, and the thick, husky murmur made her head spin until she was sinking dizzily into a warm, vibrant void as his hands urgently skimmed the curve of her hips, brushing possessively across the jut of her hip-bone and then boldly exploring the hollow of her groin beneath the silky scrap of underwear, growling deep in his throat as he eased her thighs apart to move a hard, muscular leg between her knees. The shock of this sudden, uncontrolled acceleration of events jangled a warning bell through the fog of sensation and desire, and with a muffled cry she jack-knifed beneath him, wrenching herself out of his embrace to clutch her arms around herself in a huddle of self-protection.

Nick was silent. Eventually she risked a glance at where he lay, propping himself on an arm, watching her grimly as she grappled with her dishevelled clothes to cover herself.

'*Hell*...I'm sorry...!' The husky words were deep, and tinged with such bitter self-contempt she flicked a reluctant glance at him.

'So much for your promises!' she managed to whisper furiously, aware of the illogical anger flooding through her. It took two people to ignite that sort of conflagration, and she couldn't fool herself otherwise.

'Hetti...please believe me when I tell you I didn't plan to make love to you on a public beach, like a raw teenager!' His voice was rueful, slightly ragged. 'I'm not quite sure how things got so out of hand just now...believe it or not, all I intended to do was kiss you again!'

'Well, you've kissed me again. Now I'd like to go home!'

There was a long silence, and Nick slowly sat up, leaning forward, his elbows resting on slightly bent knees, watching her intently.

'Was I way out of line, Hetti?' he probed quietly, his voice still uneven. 'Or were there just a few seconds when you wanted exactly what I wanted?'

'Nick, what I feel...my sexual feelings...none of that has anything to do with you! Just because you're my employer doesn't give you some old-fashioned droit de seigneur!'

'Forget I'm your employer for the moment, Hetti— and it's not just your sexual feelings I'm interested in, even though I patently find you desirable——' his tone was wry '—even though you're the most desirable female I've ever come across——'

'Cross me off your long list!' she cut in bleakly, thinking of his daunting reputation and shivering suddenly in the cool night air off the ocean. 'Neither of us wants a full commitment to someone else. And sex without commitment isn't my style at all...'

'How about sex with commitment?' His voice was ominously quiet.

'I'm afraid I don't follow you...' But her heart was thudding suddenly, and she gripped her fingers together tightly in front of her knees, for a split second wondering what it was he was about to say, heat flooding through her at what it *might* be...

'How was the sex in your marriage, Hetti? Was that your style?'

His words were so very far from what a secret part of her had yearned for him to say, a painful disappointment beyond her understanding brought a spasm of fury as she span abruptly to her feet. 'Mind your own damned business!' It was a half-sob as she strode rapidly past Nick's figure on the sand, and made for the car through the rapidly fading light. She heard a smothered exclamation as she left, but she refused to turn round, reaching the Alvis a few minutes later and leaning, trembling, against the bonnet.

The nerve, the sheer, persistent invasiveness of him . . . she took a deep breath, grateful for her seething temper which was overshadowing the lost, aching void inside her.

The cool night air was full of salt and honeysuckle. A bat swooped and dived against the fading of the sky. It was very lonely and very quiet, apart from the distant motion of the waves. She glanced around with a tug of apprehension. Where was he? What on earth was taking him so long? Surely, he couldn't be sitting on the beach *sulking*?

Reluctantly, she began to walk back the way she'd come, and then she saw him, sitting on the flat rock, his back to her, head bent forward, hands to his face. She stopped as she rounded the end of the path, frowning at his stance, her stomach contracting painfully. Breaking into a run, she covered the rest of the ground like lightning, her heart almost bursting as she reached his side.

'Nick? Nick, what is it? What's wrong——?' She began shakily, then stopped abruptly. 'Oh! Sand in your eyes?' For a dreadful, heart-stopping split second she'd thought he was crying, and she felt annoyed at herself for the thought. Hard macho-men like Nick Trevelyan didn't cry, especially over something as trivial as a failed sexual conquest.

'Correct. Next time you flounce off, kindly watch where you're kicking the sand, will you?' He was squinting in pain and dabbing gingerly at his eyes with a large white handkerchief.

'Oh, I'm sorry...' Biting her lip guiltily, she watched his ineffectual efforts for a few seconds, then with a low exclamation of distress she took his chin in her hand and turned his face up to her.

'Give me the handkerchief, but lick one corner,' she advised huskily, carefully pulling out the corner of each of Nick's eyes in turn and proceeding to dab and flick with an expertise born of frequent trips to the beach with the twins over the years. 'There, how does that feel?'

After a few exploratory blinks, he nodded abruptly. 'Better.' He took the handkerchief from her with a thin smile. 'The role of ministering angel seems to be your style, if nothing else, Hetti.'

She stared at him, her throat drying with the depth of her feelings in that moment, and he stared back, the pale gleam of his eyes with their fringe of thick dark lashes appearing devastatingly back to normal. With a muttered oath he stood up, pushing the handkerchief back into his waistcoat pocket, his expression brooding. The silence extended, and he seemed to be battling with his thoughts.

'You're right to feel angry with me,' he murmured at length, putting his hands on her shoulders and frowning at her involuntary flinch. 'I'm not entitled to explanations. But you can't blame me for being mystified, Hetti. When I touch you, you light up like a firework, you know damn well you do... That kind of thing plays havoc with the male libido, in case you didn't know——'

'Please, don't start again——'

'And then you freeze like a lake in winter,' he went on hoarsely, his eyes intent on her face. 'Why, Hetti?'

Something seemed to snap inside her, a vague awareness of how close she was to making a total fool of herself over this man, a kind of despairing fury at his clinical, analytical probing into her feelings. Panic-stricken, she snapped, '*Why?* Because I don't happen to want to jump into bed with my new boss and have a convenient little sex romp on the side, that's why!'

'Hetti, no one's saying you should——'

'Let me finish!' she cut in tautly. 'I didn't start any of this, you did! You... you kissed me when we were in France, and ever since then you've been subtly leaning on me, putting the pressure on! But it's just so unfair! I've got to earn my living, and I happen to be enjoying my job. On the strength of my new earnings, just like you suggested, I'm buying that little cottage up there——' she swept an arm towards Roscarrock Cottage up on the cliff '—so I don't want to lose my job in a couple of months' time, or however long it takes your numerous affairs to fizzle out!'

'There's no question of your losing your job!' He sounded as if he was suppressing his own anger with enormous difficulty.

'Oh, thanks! Big deal! But think how embarrassing it would be when our affair finished, and you were still stuck with me in your office all day? It would be embarrassing for me, too! Besides, I'd hate to cramp your celebrated style, Nick! I'd hate to get in the way of Joelle, and... *Helga*, or even, heaven forbid, *Annette*?'

It was hard to be sure in the growing dusk, but the colour seemed to have receded from Nick's dark face. He looked pale and tense and angry. 'Annette? Who the hell's been talking to you about Annette, Henrietta?'

The new ice in his voice made her blush deeply, glad there was so little light left to see by.

'Your ex-secretary Gillian was revealing all in the office last week. She told me she'd had a crush on you herself.' She related the other girl's words expressionlessly. 'In fact she said most of the females at Trevelyan Estates were madly in love with you! But Gillian realised she was wasting her time, because you'd been disillusioned forever by a fickle red-head called Annette. So she went off and found someone nice and reliable called Phillip——'

'Very wise of her,' he said curtly. 'Perceptive beyond her intelligence, in fact!' He shot a brief, glittering smile at her and began to stride rapidly up the beach, departing so abruptly she had to run to catch up with him. 'Come on, time I took you home. I wouldn't want to provide more gossip fodder than I have already!'

'Nick—I wasn't gossiping . . . believe me, I hate gossip more than anyone . . . !'

'Get in. I'll deposit you at your door, untouched by further lecherous fingers, Henrietta.' The deep voice dripped furious distaste. 'Just do me a favour in the office in future? Avoid those tight skirts and wrap-over silk blouses, otherwise you may have to get the office junior to put more bromide in my tea!'

The volume of work over the next few weeks, the frantic pace of each day's activity, did nothing to speed the hours spent, in a state of uneasy truce, side by side with Nick in the office. Not even the ceremonial collection of the keys for Roscarrock Cottage, and a surprise visit from her old friend Clare down from London to help her plan colour-schemes and scour junk shops, could dispel the shadow of the tension between herself and Nick.

'You look worn out, poppet!' Clare told her, tossing back her own sophisticated ash-blonde bob and eyeing her friend's stripy, untamed mane and darkly smudged eyes with a narrowed look of concern. 'You're overdoing things, obviously. Don't you think so, Piers?'

Piers had called in to see the progress at the cottage, and nodded sagely, eyeing Clare's model-girl legs and scarlet nails with more than a touch of male interest. 'All work and no play!' he agreed laconically. 'That's a trap you never catch me falling into!'

'Really?' Hetti turned from her laborious job of stripping layers of gloss paint from the beautiful old pine banisters, her expression wry. 'Well, you might like to know Nick's earmarked you as a potential French-speaking guide for our inspection flights to France, so you may find your hours being stepped up soon!'

'Oh, great! When I get my private pilot licence I could even fly the Cessna myself! Mind you,' Piers frowned suddenly, 'I hope there won't be too many *weekends* tied up in it...'

'Oh, that would be the limit, wouldn't it!' she agreed with pointed sarcasm. 'Since everyone seems intent on forcing their opinions on me, Piers, how about taking some of your own medicine? Choose which of your interests are more important to you, having a good time, or your career, then give it priority! Otherwise, you might just find yourself out on your ear!'

'Hmmm...touchy. Sure sign of overwork. And aligning yourself with the top brass, as well,' Piers teased, grinning at Clare as she leafed through a home-decorating book entitled *Decorating on a Budget* for cheap and cheerful ideas. 'Does this mean the rumours about you and Nick Trevelyan are true, I wonder?'

'What rumours?' She was goaded into snapping the question, and saw Clare's dusky blue eyes widen with curiosity.

'You left that musical soirée together rather suddenly, that's all. After your amazing double act, the tongues have been twittering ever since. Speculation is rife...'

'Hetti, what *have* you been up to, darling?' Clare put the magazine down and leaned forward, eyes gleaming.

'Holding the population of St Wenna spellbound with the purity of her voice, accompanied by the fantastically skilful violin playing of the one and only Nicholas Trevelyan, ex-Royal Academy of Music, brilliant career tragically halted by a brutal intervention of fate——' Piers supplied melodramatically, until Henrietta could stand no more.

'Do me a favour, Piers? Tell everyone to mind their own damned business! And that includes you!'

She slammed her pot of paint-stripper down so hard some of it splashed perilously close to her fingers, and marched upstairs, recognising her behaviour as childishly defensive the moment she reached her bedroom and flopped exhaustedly down on the bed, but quite unable to do anything to rectify the situation. The sound of the other two chatting and laughing downstairs, discussing Piers's frequent trips to London, and Clare's high-powered modelling career, did nothing to improve her seething ill humour.

It was silly to let Piers get under her skin, but somehow she couldn't help it. Clare, with the sensitivity of a friend who'd known her since they were both about ten, forebore to question her too closely during the rest of her stay. Henrietta felt deeply grateful. She wasn't sure why, but she felt vulnerable and raw inside whenever Nick's name was mentioned...

'But you know you're always welcome to come and stay with us in London, poppet,' Clare reminded her brightly, as she climbed back into her neat little MG to leave on Sunday night. 'So don't feel you've got to stick things out down here if you've had enough!'

'Thanks, Clare. I'll remember that!' She hugged her friend quickly, and watched the small red car drive off up the steep cliff road with a forlorn, abandoned feeling which persisted for several days, and made her furious with her own self-pity.

Marc Mercier's telephone call later in the week produced mixed feelings, too.

'Let me take you to that dinner you promised me! Tonight—don't say no!'

'Well, I...' She hesitated, quelling objections. She'd known the Merciers were over here; Nick had communicated that much to her, but he'd seemed disinclined to include her in any of this round of meetings and negotiations, and his cool, patronising attitude hurt. She was beginning to grow weary of his scathing mood as he prowled around the office, snarling at anyone who had the misfortune to stumble across his path. She'd discovered skills of diplomacy untested until now, as she soothed the terrified typists under her control, and prayed for a respite. But the tension was exhausting.

'I promised dinner before I realised you were married, Monsieur Mercier!' she said lightly, and heard his bluff laugh over the telephone.

'Joelle is touring your offices with Nick this afternoon. Depending on the traffic, I understand they may stay overnight somewhere—Nick did not tell you?'

She swallowed convulsively, a cold hand closing over her heart. She'd known about the tour of the offices, of course, and that the far-flung locations and narrow Cornish lanes made an overnight stay a pleasant option, but naïvely she'd assumed Marc was going with them . . .

'Yes, yes, of course I knew.'

'I stayed behind to talk with Nick's company lawyers.' Marc's voice was bland, and she pulled herself together with a supreme effort, distantly hearing herself agreeing to meet him for dinner at eight in a cool, detached tone quite unlike her normal one, while an icy pain grew and expanded inside her until she felt quite numb.

The pain didn't lessen, even after a pleasant meal on the terrace of a local hotel. It didn't help that it was the same hotel, the Trebarnock Cove, where Nick had taken her for a meal that first night, after the interview . . . the memories of that evening with Nick seemed to increase her closed-up, agonised introspection. She was oblivious to Marc's amusing conversation, and flattering attention. Throughout the evening she had a searing mental picture of Nick and Joelle, sitting at some cosy, candlelit table somewhere, Joelle's blue eyes devouring him over their meal, the notion of them going up to some luxurious hotel room afterwards, of Nick's lean brown hands making love to Joelle with that same glorious, plundering urgency she'd experienced on the beach that night . . . it made her feel as if someone were kicking her in the stomach.

'I'd invite you in for coffee, Marc,' she turned a pale shadow of a smile to him at the end of the evening, 'but I'm still in the throes of moving in. There's nowhere to sit, and pots of paint everywhere. But thanks for a lovely evening. Sorry I've been such poor company . . .'

'Nonsense, you've been charming company. Perhaps...a little preoccupied?' he admitted, grinning ruefully. 'There is something on your mind, Henrietta, perhaps something I could help with?' There was a note in his bland voice which made her turn quickly to look at him.

'Marc—I've no right to ask you this, but...your marriage to Joelle...are you happy together?'

He gazed at her thoughtfully, then began to laugh softly..He was fingering the ignition key of the hired Jaguar, eyeing the dark windows of her cottage speculatively.

'Is this a hopeful sign? Do you wish to discover if I am available for liaisons on the side?'

'No!'

There'd been a tinge of mockery in his voice which told her he didn't really expect her to take him seriously.

'No, I thought not. I am not the man you would like to invite up to your bedroom with you, am I?'

'I'm not in the habit of asking any man up to my bedroom on the strength of one meal out!'

'Quite. So, when you ask about my marriage, *cherie*, it is because you wish to know if Nick Trevelyan and my wife Joelle are in love with each other, *d'accord*?'

'Marc, I'm sorry...I shouldn't have started this conversation...'

Her palms suddenly felt damp, and she wiped them shakily on the floral skirt of her suit, finding it hard to believe any man could speak so dispassionately about the possibility of his wife loving another man!

'No—please, Henrietta. You are in love with Nick, so it is natural that you should want to know——'

'That's not true!' she burst out passionately, horrified. 'I'm not in love with Nick!'

'Listen, Henrietta. I suspect that you are a romantic. You think true love lasts for all time . . . but not everyone sees life like that. Joelle and I co-exist. Our passion is long past. Our business and the wishes of our families deter us from divorcing. But we lead our own lives. Do you understand?'

She gave a stifled exclamation, and fumbled for the door handle, not wanting to hear any more, but Marc had the air of a man warming to his theme.

'I believe Joelle is wasting her energies on Nick. If this is any consolation, I suspect Nick is a man who avoids commitment to one woman . . .'

Suddenly she was riveted to her seat again. She wanted to escape, but she was quite unable to tear herself away from Marc's revelations.

'This may seem strange to you,' he continued, 'but I respect Nick. We are on the same wavelength, *tu comprends*? I understand what motivates him. Life has taught him to be cautious, defensive—his insistence on driving, for example, is because of the car crash when his brother was killed, you knew that?'

'I . . . I . . . yes. I knew about the car crash.' It was a ragged whisper.

'I think, too, that life has taught him to be equally cautious in his personal life, cautious in his relationships with women. *Je crois que c'est vrai. Et toi?*'

'I . . .'

'Yet in business he is bold, adventurous, makes quick decisions, takes risks . . . he is shrewd, and this is what I respect in a businessman. I respect Nick, wish to do business with him, whether or not he may be sleeping with my wife. Do you find this hard to understand, *ma petite*?'

'Yes, very hard to understand...' She couldn't take any more of this amoral cynicism. She felt sick. Pinning a brave, bright smile on her face, she scrambled out of the car before he could witness a humiliating breakdown in control. 'Thanks for the meal, Marc.'

With a choked goodnight, she fled inside and slammed the heavy oak front door, standing quite still in the darkness, listening to the pounding of her own heart, the uneven catch of her breathing as she fought for control.

There was a small armchair in the sitting-room, and she picked her way blindly over and sat down, lifting trembling hands to her face. For once she was oblivious to the view from her window, uncaring of the rippling waves in the moonlight far below. She was fighting a silent battle inside, fighting the shivers beginning to course through her body.

She was in love with Nick, Marc had said. It hadn't been a question, but a statement.

Misery engulfed her, a great wave of pain and confusion. Marc's twisted philosophy of life had left a nasty taste in her mouth, his outlook so alien she felt suddenly bewildered and very alone. An unreal feeling swept over her. Stiffly she made her way upstairs, to stare at herself in the wardrobe mirror, as if her reflection might answer some formless, panicky question inside her.

She looked wraithlike in the semi-darkness, the blue and cream flowery suit hanging loose in places it would previously have clung, showing where she'd lost weight in the last few weeks. Her heavy brindled mane of hair framed an oval face too white and drawn, but in what felt like a moment of heightened awareness, as if she'd taken a drug that had altered her perception and perspective, tilted her whole angle of looking at things, her features looked at once familiar and totally different. The wide-apart brown eyes looked darker, held a knowledge which in some strange, disconcerting way altered her appearance. The freckles on her turned-up nose stood out against her pallor...her wide, full mouth had an air of trembling vulnerability which made her breath catch in her throat...

And she saw it now, as if the protective barriers were collapsing like a line of dominoes. What Marc had said was true.

She reversed on to the bed, and sat down abruptly. It was true...and it hurt, horribly. She'd fallen in love with a self-possessed cynic, a man whose dissipated lifestyle included adultery with another man's wife while calmly striking a business deal, a man whose arrogance assumed that his new secretary should automatically provide sexual favours whenever required, a man who freely admitted his contempt for emotional commitment... A man whose powerful sexual appetite filled her with a dread she still hadn't fully come to terms with...

Facing the truth didn't appear to make anything simpler, it made everything much, much more complicated.

If she'd felt vulnerable before, now she felt afraid to go into the office in the morning, terrified in case that cool, penetrating green gaze read her thoughts and her heart, took cynical advantage...

But she needn't have worried about keeping her secret. The expression in Nick's eyes, when he eventually put in a late appearance at the office, was not so much coolly penetrating as a furious glitter of rage.

'What the *hell* did you think you were doing last night?' he exploded, slamming the office door shut behind him with a crash which must have resounded all over the building, and sent the already cowed typists downstairs into a fresh paroxysm of apprehension. He looked overpoweringly large and intimidating, the conventional formality of dark suit and snowy white shirt failing to tame his appearance.

'What on earth are you talking about?' Her frosty tone served only to fan his temper. With a sinking, sick feeling she watched the darkly tanned face tighten into a harsh mask of fury, the scars on temple and cheek standing out starkly white.

'You heard me! When I require you to accept dinner invitations from business contacts, I'll let you know!'

Snatching a shallow, shaky breath, she matched his glare with a scorching one of her own. 'Don't speak to me like that! What I do in my spare time is my own affair, Nick——'

'Not with my business contacts, it's not!' he ground out ferociously. 'I needed you last night, and I discovered you were out on the bloody town, wining and dining with Marc Mercier!'

'While you were staying overnight in some snug country hotel, making mad passionate love to his wife?' She flushed crimson as she said it, but almost simultaneously the colour drained from Nick's face.

The silence was resounding. The gaunt stare he fixed on her made her pulses race.

'I pay you to act as my personal secretary, not as a guardian of my morals!' he grated softly.

She stared at him in growing bewilderment, suddenly realising that his fury appeared to be totally irrational. This outburst couldn't possibly stem from an innocent meal out with Marc last night. Even in her present confused state she couldn't believe Nick would be *that* petty...

'Why did you need me last night?' she demanded shakily, when the tense silence had become unbearable. 'What's happened to put you in this foul temper, Nick?'

He turned abruptly away, presenting a broad, implacable back as he walked stiffly to the office window. He stared down at the busy street below, his profile taut, appearing to be struggling angrily with his own thoughts. When the telephone shrilled through the deadly silence, Henrietta jumped nervously, and grabbed the receiver, grateful for the diversion. 'Mr Trevelyan's office...'

'Hetti, it's Piers. Is he there?'

'Yes, hold on. I'll get him——'

'No! I don't want to speak to him—I gather you haven't yet heard the scintillating news?'

'What news?'

'As of last night, I no longer work for the cold-blooded bastard. I don't suppose *you* had a hand in any of this, sister dear? Was your little outburst last weekend an unofficial verbal warning, by any chance?'

'What? Piers, what are you talking about?' Her fingers had turned white on the receiver. 'Have you resigned?'

'No, I didn't resign.' Piers gave a light, bitter laugh. 'I've been sacked, Hetti—for professional misconduct!'

'Oh, Piers! But why? How—oh, how could you think *I* might have something to do with it? What happened?' She felt hot all over now, anger burning inside her. She glared at Nick in furious disbelief as Piers unfolded his tale of woe.

'He rolled up yesterday afternoon with Joelle Mercier...'

Even as Piers said this, the door opened and Joelle Mercier walked into the office, her supple slenderness emphasised by a saxe-blue silk designer suit, short-skirted and plunge-necked, looking supremely satisfied and assured, taking in the tense scene with lazy interest.

The sight of her distracted Henrietta so much, she had to concentrate hard on what Piers was saying.

'...then he sent her off to inspect a couple of houses while he picked through the order books and sales figures, called me a parasite, accused me of professional incompetence over the sale of that blasted cottage of yours, and of trying to put him out of bloody business! Lord knows what I'm going to do, I'm up to my eyes in credit accounts...' He laughed again, the hollow sound making her heart contract in sympathy. 'The BMW will have to go back, I suppose. I'll probably have to sell the new flat, too. Amy's far from thrilled about the whole thing, so she'll probably walk out soon——'

'Piers, just a minute—things can't be quite that bad, surely——'

'Can't they? What a naïve little thing you are, Hett. I'll talk to you later—I'm sure the callous bastard's working you like a slave. I'll fill you in on all the details when I see you. *Ciao!*'

She dropped the phone back on the hook, and met Nick's narrowed gaze with a mounting fury which made her tremble all over. Joelle's presence, propped as she was against the end of Nick's desk with the air of someone with a right to be there, made things even worse.

'You've heard the sob story?' Nick's deep voice was devoid of emotion. Hands thrust in his pockets, he gazed at her levelly, a muscle working in his cheek the only sign of underlying tension.

'Is it true?' she demanded unsteadily, her voice rising in anger. 'You've sacked my brother?'

'Yes.'

'So this is why you needed me last night? To tell me you were ruining my brother's career?'

'That's not precisely how I'd have put it——'

'Piers is nothing better than a common criminal,' Joelle purred softly. 'He has been pocketing commissions, stealing from your company——'

'You're lying!' Henrietta almost choked. 'Piers wouldn't do anything like that!' Her heart was pounding so hard she felt almost faint.

'All right, Joelle, I'll handle this,' Nick cut in quietly, receiving a slightly defensive glance from the Frenchwoman in return. 'Hetti, Piers needed a short, sharp shock today——'

'Really? You mean he's just had his whole career ruined out of... out of *vindictiveness* and... and *spite*!'

'Don't be bloody ridiculous!' Nick said icily, the cold flash of anger in his green eyes revealing the immense control he was exerting over his temper. 'You don't think I'd sack your brother out of spite?'

'Why shouldn't I think that? You certainly haven't won any medals for *altruism*! What a shame I was out enjoying myself with Marc, when I could have been treated to a much more amusing evening watching you wreck another man's life!'

'I doubt if giving your brother his marching orders will wreck his life; on the contrary, it could teach him a valuable lesson, Henrietta—maybe he'll think twice in future before breaking the law.'

She faced him, breathing jerkily, the first red-hot haze of anger fading sufficiently for questions to start forming in her head. The sudden, appalling realisation that Piers might really have committed some criminal offence brought an icy cold fear to her stomach. Surely... *surely*

Piers couldn't have been so crazy...? She stared, white-faced, at Nick, willing it to be a nightmare...

'Breaking the law?'

'Piers has cheated my firm. He's cost me fees I should have been receiving, he's been failing to give accurate, professional advice, and he's also down-valued a property and then bought it himself for a quick profit——'

'But—but he wouldn't...I know Piers...he just *wouldn't*...'

'See how frightened she looks?' Joelle murmured, flicking a long blue gaze at Nick. 'I told you, they're in it together. The whole family are clearly not to be trusted, *chéri*...'

In the aghast silence which followed this, Nick looked savagely at his watch and then fixed Joelle with an unreadable gaze.

'Joelle, this is a private matter. Leave us, please.'

Henrietta hardly saw the woman glide triumphantly out of the office, she was staring, ashen-cheeked, at Nick, tears beginning to roll unheeded down her face.

'Is that what you think? That whatever it is Piers is alleged to have done, that he and I are in *league* together?' It was a harsh, agonised whisper.

Nick's dark face was thunderous, his eyes glittering with a fresh fury.

'Stop looking at me like that!' he growled. 'How the hell do I know? All I know is I'm sick of being made to feel guilty, by you and your blasted brother! I'm running a business, not a charitable trust! I'm trying to finalise an important set-up in France—I need this fiasco like a hole in the head!'

She spun on her heel, abruptly.

'Where the hell do you think you're going now?'

'I'm going to see Piers, find out from him exactly what's been going on...' She was marching back to her own office as she spoke. Nick followed her, his tone still rough with fury.

'Maybe you should listen to me, first!'

'No!' she burst out, all the pent-up frustration and misery of the last few weeks erupting in the savage refusal. 'I'd rather hear the truth from my own brother than a pack of malicious lies from *you*!'

She stormed to the outer door and turned briefly before she left, fighting the treacherous tears which threatened to dissolve fury to despair.

'Don't wait around for me to come back—as far as I'm concerned, I'm resigning right now! And I hope I never have to see you again!'

The office door crashed closed after her, the resounding echo almost as violent as the one heralding Nick's arrival a few minutes earlier.

CHAPTER EIGHT

Two weeks later, Henrietta pushed the key into the lock of the tiny pink-painted mews house in the quiet heart of Belgravia, and let herself into the refreshing coolness of the hall. The hot summer weather seemed to be going on forever, and while it would no doubt be wonderful down in the fresh sea air of Cornwall, the heat in the city was suffocating to work in.

'Clare? I'm back!' She tossed her shoulder-bag on the floor by the coat-stand, and went wearily upstairs to the first-floor sitting-room.

'Hi! You're late! Another tough day at the word processor?'

'You could say that. Thank heaven it's Friday, as the old saying goes.' Henrietta grimaced at her friend and flopped exhaustedly on to the Regency striped sofa, kicking off her shoes immediately. 'I'm not sure which is worse, the job, or the getting there and getting back again! Quite apart from the fact that I can't sponge off you and Martin much longer, I'll have to get a bedsit nearer my office. This rush-hour stint is nearly killing me!'

She wiggled her aching feet and leaned her head back, closing her eyes. Her head ached too. And her back. In fact she ached all over.

'Hetti, you're not sponging off anyone. You're paying rent for your room, just like you would in someone else's house,' Clare informed her calmly. 'And you know how

Martin feels about you swanning around London on your own!'

'Martin is a very dear friend, Clare, but he knows I need independence.' Henrietta rubbed her forehead with her fingers, and winced at the sharp jab of pain between her eyes. 'And since he's not here to perform his big brother act at present, I intend to start bedsit-hunting in earnest this weekend!'

'Really?' Her friend's voice was wry as she flicked her eyes over Henrietta's prone form on the sofa. 'Frankly, poppet, you don't look as if you could hunt the thimble, let alone a bedsit.' Flicking the remote-control button to silence the early evening chat show on the television, Clare stood up, flapping her fingers to dry her newly applied polish, fixing her with a frown. 'I wish Martin wasn't away, or I could get out of this weekend modelling assignment—I've got a sneaky feeling you're going to go down with flu or something, and there'll be no one here to bring you aspirins and hot toddies!'

'Don't be ridiculous,' Henrietta protested weakly. 'First off, if Martin wasn't away I wouldn't have a bedroom to borrow, and camping out on the spare bed in *your* bedroom again is totally out of the question, since you snore like a tractor—— '

'I do *not*!'

'And secondly, no one goes down with the flu in this weather!'

'Maybe, but you've definitely gone a nasty pasty colour!'

'Thanks a lot!' With a supreme effort, Henrietta sat up straight on the sofa, and forced a bright smile. 'We can't all look like Vogue cover-girls, remember! Some of us get frayed around the edges after a heavy day in the office!'

'Ouch!' Clare laughed. 'Straight between the eyes! I'll have you know the modelling world has plenty of gruelling moments, Henrietta Beauman!' She saw the slight flicker in Henrietta's eyes at her use of her maiden name, and grimaced. 'Sorry...I keep forgetting your name is Melyn!'

'Don't worry—I've got over being ultra-sensitive about that.'

Clare sat down again, eyeing her thoughtfully. 'Have you, Hett? Really?'

Henrietta stared at her friend bleakly for a long moment, then shrugged. 'As far as it's possible to. I'm not sure how much one can ever forget something like that...or whether it'll ever be possible to stop feeling guilty...'

'Guilty?' Clare demanded disbelievingly. 'Hetti, darling, what do you have to feel guilty about?'

'About...oh, all of it!' She massaged the back of her aching neck with her fingers, feeling the unfamiliar bareness where her newly cut bob left her nape exposed. 'The fault wasn't all on Tristan's side—we were both involved in the decision to marry each other, after all! I just wish...I just wish I could have been there when he needed me...oh, heavens, just listen to me!' she finished up with a grimace. 'Bemoaning my lot all over again! The trouble with me is I'm just not good company any more. It can't be much fun being lumbered with a misery like me!'

She pulled a comical face at Clare, who shook her head in impatient disagreement.

'You're not a misery. You're one of my oldest friends, and you've had a tough time recently. And if you want the harsh truth from someone who knew Tristan nearly as well as you did, darling, Tris was a spoilt youngest child of a wealthy family. He didn't know *what* he needed.'

'Maybe that's what we had in common! We were both spoilt youngest children—or at least I was until the twins arrived on the scene. Hopefully I've grown up a bit in the last few years, but I'm still mixed up and confused— I don't know what I need either!' Henrietta said flatly. 'But I know what I don't need, that's for sure. I *don't* need any more involvements with the opposite sex! It's not an area I'm ever likely to have much success in...'

'Well, before you consider applying for a nunnery, make sure you sort out your feelings for the dishy Nick Trevelyan! Because from what Piers has been telling me, he's been a broken man since you marched out on him!'

Henrietta went very still, and there was an awkward silence for several minutes.

'What exactly *has* Piers been telling you, Clare?'

'Don't look so tragic and *betrayed*, Hetti dear!' Clare raised her eyebrows unrepentantly. 'No one's been colluding behind your back or anything! Piers just happened to mention something about it when he rang the other evening and you weren't back from the office...' She saw Henrietta's cool stare, and shrugged slightly. 'He said that Nick Trevelyan seems to be in a permanent black mood, and that the mention of your name produces an even more ferocious temper than normal!'

'Nick Trevelyan is just a naturally foul-tempered person,' Henrietta said, closing her eyes and trying to will her headache to vanish. 'And there's nothing to sort out with him.'

'You have to admit, though, darling...your abrupt exit ran true to past form—it was a touch on the impulsive side.' Clare spoke gently, but there was a gleam of affectionate amusement in her eyes. 'It strikes me as immensely ironic that you march out in protest at Piers's being sacked, and Nick Trevelyan promptly checks up on him, gives him a man-to-man talk, reinstates him and gives him a second chance!'

'Didn't you say you were being collected at seven-thirty?'

Clare suddenly noticed the clock and gave a squeak of dismay. 'Gosh, it's past that now—Justin will be here any second!'

In a last-minute whirl of forgotten gear and exuberant warnings to have a quiet couple of days, Clare gave her a hug then frowned again at the dark smudges and strained pallor of Henrietta's face.

'Have a quiet, restful weekend,' Clare ordered, twirling round as the doorbell rang to announce her photographer Justin's arrival, and, grabbing her cases and make-up bags ready to dash downstairs, flicked her a last apprehensive glance. 'Are you *sure* you're OK?'

'I'm fine, honestly. Nothing an early night won't cure. Stop fussing—you're beginning to sound like Helen!'

'Then I'll see you on Sunday night... Bye, darling...'

'Yes—see you Sunday night.' The slam of the front door announced Clare's departure, and Henrietta went up to her bedroom, her legs like lead, her headache growing progressively worse, until the only thing she could think of to do was swallow a couple of aspirins and fall into bed, furious with herself at such a display of frailty.

The morning brought a slight improvement, but the weight of her head as she struggled to lift it off the pillow confirmed her worst suspicions. She didn't think people were supposed to get the flu in a heatwave, but she appeared to have something uncannily like it!

She picked up the phone to ring the friend she'd been due to attend a concert with. Even if she dosed herself on aspirins and felt up to going by tonight, her friend might not take kindly to the risk of catching it. Besides, she wasn't really in the mood for going out. She wasn't in the mood for seeing or doing anything. The way she felt right now, if a large black hole in the ground opened and conveniently swallowed her up, she wouldn't give it a second thought.

There was an answerphone recording calls, and she left a brief message, then collapsed on the sofa, feeling utterly spent. The next two days stretched ahead, with the house empty and the sensation of the city around her buzzing with people about to hit the high life for the weekend, and she felt her inner emptiness growing, expanding, until the aching sense of loss became unbearable...

Which was farcical, she reminded herself sternly, sipping the mug of scalding tea she'd managed to make, and swallowing another aspirin, because in spite of the ultimate outcome of the Piers incident, she'd only done what she wanted to do, what she'd felt compelled to do; her commitment to staying in Cornwall had been impossible, for lots of different reasons. Tristan, her family, Nick Trevelyan... but mainly Nick Trevelyan... The thought of Joelle's triumphant presence in the office that last morning, of her obvious rapport with Nick, made her feel sick with misery... and that scathing condemnation of herself and Piers, even the whole family, still seethed inside her—in spite of subsequent events.

'If you ask me, in a peculiar, roundabout sort of way, this could be the making of Piers! We all owe Nick Trevelyan a vote of thanks!' had been Helen's ascerbic comment, appearing to reflect the Beauman family's opinion when she said it.

And Piers himself, when he'd come up to see her two days after she arrived in London, had been unbelievably remorseful in the cold light of day, and dedicated to putting his life in order.

'I've been a bloody fool,' he had told her simply. 'Nick's made me see that. Throwing money around like water, trying to impress Amy...the trouble was, once I started telling her I earned a fortune, I had to keep it up! Do you understand, Hett? Oh, lord, the flying lessons, the weekends away with the county sets—nothing comes cheap these days, does it?' He had raked his blond hair from his eyes with an impatient gesture. 'I don't deserve a second chance! Nick could have called in the bloody fraud squad or something, if he'd wanted!'

'No, you *don't* deserve a second chance!' she'd told him angrily. 'And, just for the record, were you actually ripping me off over Roscarrock Cottage, Piers?'

He had shaken his head, and had the grace to blush slightly. 'No, Roscarrock Cottage was a genuine mistake on my part—I clean forgot to reveal my relationship with *you* to Mrs Chivell. That's initially what Nick picked me up on—he was angry enough about that! Under the Estate Agency Act, failing to divulge a relationship with a purchaser could get the agent sued for malpractice! Then he started digging deeper, and discovered I'd quoted a discounted commission for a cash deal on another big house in Hone, and pocketed the money...I hadn't put the sale through the books. That little fraud stood me in at a fairly substantial four-figure sum! It paid for the BMW, at least...'

'Piers, I *despair* of you! How *could* you? I thought you admired Nick Trevelyan, hero-worshipped him even? How could you behave like that, as an employee?'

Piers had shaken his head, with a groan. 'Hero-worship? You make me sound like an adolescent. But, yes, it's partly true. I've always looked up to him, wanted to emulate him, never quite had enough money to do it! Hetti, I've learned my lesson, I promise you that! I'm repaying the money I defrauded out of my salary over the next twelve months. And, let's face it, Nick's hardly going to let me out of his sight from now on! I'm *bound* to be a reformed character, by the time he's finished with me! I'm just really sorry you threw in your job on account of it all, Hetti love...'

Henrietta closed her eyes, the ache intensifying, the misery threatening to rise and swallow her up, and the rest of the day was spent scanning the papers for bedsits, short-listing the possibles, trying frantically to keep going, and failing miserably, until at last she collapsed in a shivering heap and fought off the growing panic that inactivity of any description invariably brought.

The truth was, since she'd stormed out of Nick's office just two weeks ago, she'd sailed through each day with flying colours, the whole thing strictly under control, as long as she kept going. She'd placed Roscarrock Cottage in the hands of another estate agent for holiday rentals, and to her amazement it was already fully booked up until the end of October. The extra income from that helped pay the mortgage, and she could always hope for a longer-term letting during the winter months. The job she'd found quite easily in an estate agent's office in Camberwell was dull and boring compared with her work for Nick, but it was all she could cope with at present. She hadn't had time to hunt for another high-powered position, anyway, and this was more a run-of-the-mill job where she could hide and lick her wounds and try to come to terms with her feelings.

And she hadn't retired into a shell, sunk into depression—she'd made what her mother would have termed 'a determined effort' to cheer herself up. With Clare's encouragement, she'd had her hair cut into this fashionable bob, experimented with new make-up, been shopping and bought new clothes. She'd accepted invitations from her colleagues at work, as well as going out with Clare, and other mutual friends, and with Martin. She'd been swimming and to the theatre, done all the things females were supposed to do to mend a broken heart...

As long as she kept busy, it was all right. It was when she stopped that the pain began, and the pain was so immense she had no way of handling it, except by crumpling into a pathetic wreck. And that was exactly what she didn't intend to become. She'd been there once before, albeit for different reasons and with a different intensity—but the experience had left her wary of a repeat performance...

Closing her eyes, she stopped trying to rationalise. It was hopeless, even when she was feeling bright and alert. At present, with this humdinger of a headache, it was a complete waste of time.

In the hope that it would bring down her temperature, she took a cool shower, but the result was such an agonising bout of the shivers that she crawled into bed with her long white Victorian nightdress huddled around her, and let the bug do its worst.

She slept, she wasn't sure how long, eventually jerking awake in the throes of a disturbing dream to hear the doorbell ringing insistently down in the hall. It was all she could do to gather her wits together, and stumble down to open it, trying to work out the time. The fever seemed to have broken, but she still felt ridiculously wobbly. The hall clock showed it was only half-past seven—surely her friend hadn't cancelled her evening out to call and see how she was?

'Didn't you get my message?' she croaked, as she swung open the door, then stopped abruptly, her heart jolting in her chest, and a sick churning beginning in her stomach.

For a few seconds she felt as if she'd stopped breathing and would have to work really hard at starting again, then with a long, shuddering breath she focused warily on Nick's face.

'Can I come in?' He sounded harsh, distant, and without waiting for her permission he stepped inside the shadowy hall, overpoweringly attractive in denim jeans and loose denim shirt, leather jacket slung over his shoulder. His eyes were bleakly sardonic as he glanced briefly around him, then took in her dishevelled appearance in the crumpled nightdress.

'What are you doing here, Nick?'

'I was flying up to London on business,' he said flatly, raking her bitterly with his eyes. 'I had a masochistic urge to drop by and see where you ran away to this time!'

'*This* time? You talk as if I make a habit of running away!' Her voice didn't sound quite like her own. She swallowed hard and forced her eyes to meet his with an attempt at steadiness.

'Don't you?' He stared down at her in angry silence, and she hugged her arms around herself as the cooler evening air blew in through the open front door. She wished the hall wasn't so dark, so that she could see his face, but she shrank from putting on the light.

'Nothing's changed, I see,' she retorted finally, trying to control her shivering. 'I haven't seen you for two weeks, and we're into the insults already!'

'I seem to remember you called me a few unpleasant names the last time we were together... but I'm not intending to insult you—I'm just trying to get you to face up to a few home truths! You've spent your whole life running away, because you're too frightened, or too immature, to face up to things!' The glitter of anger was just discernible in the harsh, shadowy lines of his face. 'You ran away with Tristan, presumably because your parents had forbidden it, and that was a red rag to a very spoilt little bull! Then when your marriage didn't suit you either, you ran away from that! And when you couldn't handle what was going on between *us*, you bolted again!'

He glanced coldly around him, his mouth derisive.

'And this is your favourite bolt-hole. I must say I'm intrigued to meet this Martin Harvey—he must be quite a guy to put up with his on-off affair with you!'

'Get out of here, Nick.'

'Don't look so terrorised, Henrietta.' His voice held that ominous softness she remembered only too well, and she took a step backwards, feeling for the wall to support her weight which felt in danger of growing too great for her legs.

'I just wanted a rational conversation with you—I imagined the coast would be clear enough at seven-thirty in the evening, but I can see I'm interrupting something. Sorry to get you out of bed—by all means get back upstairs to lover-boy—I wish you joy of each other...'

She was gazing at him uncomprehendingly, until his meaning sank in and she had to choke down an urge to laugh hysterically. 'Oh, yes, you're definitely interrupting something...' she began on a gasp of bitter mirth, leaning against the wall, unable to control the convulsive shivering any longer; it was racking her body so that her teeth began to chatter. Nick's expression had darkened ominously, and she glared back at him with a feverish impatience, longing for him to leave so she could crawl unhindered back to bed. 'Have you finished the moral lecture, or are you planning to keep me standing here in the hall all night while you preach your hypocritical speeches? I think the heat wave must be breaking—I'm freezing!'

With a low, uncouth swear-word under his breath, he bent to examine her more closely, then found the light-switch and flicked it on, taking in her strained pallor with a ferocious frown. 'In hell's name...you're ill! What the *devil* are you doing opening the front door? Some lover-boy you've picked yourself, letting you walk around in this state!'

There was a tortured sound to his voice, but without waiting for her reply he swept her up into his arms, crushed her against the steady beating of his heart through the rough texture of his shirt. 'Where's your bedroom?' he snapped.

'I...s...second floor, but I can walk there... If I managed to walk down the stairs I can walk back up again...'

Ignoring her, he shouldered his way up two flights of stairs, carrying her as if she were as light as a child, then paused on the landing.

'Which one?'

'In there...'

Nick kicked open the door she had pointed a shaky finger towards, jaw tightening as he saw the wide double bed, noted the masculine colours of the deep navy curtains, the mole-brown and blue bedcovers and carpet. But he lay her on the bed with a surprising gentleness, and drew the duvet over her shivering body.

'Have you seen a doctor?'

'Don't be silly, it's just a touch of flu. I'm over it now, the fever's nearly gone...'

'When did you last take an analgesic?'

'I...I took two aspirins a few hours ago...I think...' She put a trembling hand to her head, trying to clear her thoughts, a feat proving doubly difficult with Nick's disturbing presence sitting on the edge of her bed. 'I had a cold shower to bring my temperature down...I don't like taking too many tablets...but it didn't work too well, so I got into bed and fell asleep. You woke me ringing the doorbell...'

'So you're alone? Where's Martin Harvey?'

'My *lover-boy*?' she demanded unevenly. 'Martin is away on a business course. And Clare is on a modelling assignment this weekend——'

'Clare?'

'Martin's sister. An old school-friend of mine. She lives here, she and Martin share the house—it was left to them both by a rich auntie. Now, if you've finished the third degree, I'd quite like to be left in peace!'

'I'm sorry...' His deep voice held a terse note of pity, and she had to bite her lip hard to quell a ridiculous urge to howl like a baby at the least hint of softening in his attitude. 'I'm not exactly helping, am I?' Nick thrust a shaking hand through his dark hair, staring at her with gaunt, haunted eyes. 'Stay in bed. I'll go and get you something.'

She lay in bed while he disappeared, unable to think straight, but the burning ache inside her seemed to have no connection with the remains of the fever heating her skin and throbbing through her skull, but more to do with the lingering after-effects of being carried so tightly in his arms, and laid so gently into bed . . .

'How do you feel now?' He'd brought her some more aspirins, and a cup of tea.

'Apart from someone pumping my arms and legs full of concrete, and tying a lead weight around my head, you mean? Fine, thanks.'

'You look different—you've had your hair cut, you've lost weight . . .' His eyes were tortured with such furious intensity she felt a wave of reaction flooding through her.

'You mean I look scraggy and shorn?' It was a failed attempt at humour, but she found herself staring at him hungrily, the misery of the past two weeks thrown into stark contrast with the illogical joy of seeing him again. She loved him . . . she still loved him . . . and she realised she'd never loved anyone the way she loved Nick . . .

Suddenly it didn't matter whether he'd been having an affair with Joelle, it didn't matter about Piers, it didn't even matter that he thought she was sleeping with Martin, it didn't even matter if he only wanted a casual fling with her until he tired of her . . . The pain darkening his eyes at this moment, the odd look of vulnerability touching the harsh lines of his features . . . there was an answering pain inside her, too agonising to ignore . . .

In that split second, she knew, with total certainty, that whatever the outcome she had to give herself the chance to explore this fragile pain inside her; she had to allow herself the courage to risk being hurt again . . .

After a long silence, he gave a grim, bitter half-smile. 'No. The diet may have been a mistake, but I like the hairstyle.'

She hadn't been dieting, she wanted to say, the kilos had just been falling off her ever since she left Cornwall ... but somehow she couldn't form the words.

'Drink some tea.'

She took a shaky sip, registering that it was just the right strength in spite of her decimated taste-buds, and to her horror she heard herself saying calmly, 'Nick, you don't need to hang around, you know—I'm fine now. And I'm quite sure you've better ways of spending your weekend than playing nursemaid to an ex-secretary you don't even *like* very much.'

'Don't be bloody silly.'

'What's that supposed to mean?' The lightness of her tone scarcely hid the shake in her voice, or the sudden rapid drumming of her heart. 'That you actually *want* to be here?'

He stood up, his eyes bleak and haunted. 'Hetti, I've been doing my damnedest not to write you off as a fickle, perfidious little bitch ... don't undo all my efforts and twist the knife in the wound!'

Her heart jolted abruptly. She was crazy, she told herself to no avail—she must be bent on self-destruction... Nick, of all the men she could have picked, was the very *last* man on earth she should offer her pathetic, fragile little gift of trust ... she'd be better off in that convent she'd joked about to Clare ...

'I don't understand—what do you want, Nick?' she whispered shakily.

'What do I *want*? I *wanted* you, more than I've ever wanted a woman in my life! Then you made your opinion of me brutally obvious, and just in case I didn't get the message loud and clear you came back to resume your affair with Martin Harvey to ram it home once and for all ...'

No—that's not true... The words she wanted to say were tangled up somewhere inside her, but they wouldn't come out.

'So you're right,' he continued icily, turning towards the door. 'I do have better things to do. So if you're feeling better, Hetti, I'll cut along now... because quite frankly my idea of an enjoyable weekend is definitely not seeing you, all demure and mock-virginal in that white nightdress, lying there in another man's bed!'

CHAPTER NINE

'NICK...!' He'd left the room, was halfway down the stairs before Henrietta found the coherence to call his name. When he didn't stop, she hurled herself out of bed, across the bedroom and on to the landing.

'*Nick!* Oh, Nick, don't go. I don't care if you don't want me any more, I don't care what you think of me, but don't go...please don't go!'

It was a terrified sob, wrenched from her very soul, and tears were welling up unheeded and pouring down her face as she clutched on to the banisters, willing her legs to support her. He'd stopped, stiff and tense, on the lower landing, and very slowly he turned back to look at her, his hard face paler beneath his tan. She began to follow him, clinging to the banister rail, suddenly so overcome with weakness that every atom in her body seemed to be involved in the vital concentration needed to stay on her feet, not to collapse in an ignominious heap on the floor.

'Hetti...oh, lord...Hetti...' He came back up the stairs two at a time, and snatched her hungrily against him before she swayed and fell. She let go of the banister rail and locked her arms around his neck, her fingers threading through his hair, holding on to him as if her life depended on it. With a muffled exclamation he crushed her closer, his hands moulding her slender body under the light cotton, his caresses growing more urgent as she melted against him in abrupt, mindless, total surrender.

He lifted her and carried her back up to the wide double bed, and when he hesitated she caught his arm, pulling him down to her.

'Hetti...'

'Please don't hate me,' she whispered chokingly against his mouth, and felt him tighten his arms round her convulsively.

'Hate you? I'm crazy about you, damn you.' It was a thick, despairing groan. 'I want you so much it's slowly killing me...'

'And I want you...' was her husky whisper, the tentative caresses of her hands making him catch his breath roughly.

With dark, questioning eyes he searched her face, then crushed her tightly against him, his lips on her face and eyes and hair, his hands moving hungrily over her.

'Hetti...oh, *Hetti*...'

She melted against him, her softness yielding to the angular strength of his body as he peeled away the nightdress and flung his own clothes haphazardly to the floor, drawing back only to stare at her as she lay, exposed and vulnerable, beneath him. The blaze of male possessiveness she saw in his eyes as they roamed over the pale beauty of her breasts, down over the smoothness of her abdomen and the slightness of her hips, lingering on the secret dark V at her groin, made her catch her breath involuntarily.

'I've wanted to do this for so long...you're so beautiful...'

'So are you...' It was a shy, throaty whisper, as she lifted her fingers to trace the scars on temple and lip, then dared to let her eyes follow the same path his had taken, a great surge of heat beginning to shimmer through her at the sight of his arousal.

'Make love to me... Please, I want you to...' It was torn impatiently, unevenly from her before he took her mouth with his, his hands in her hair, then sliding shudderingly down her body to explore the soft curves and hollows, lowering himself on to her so that they were crushed together, taking her down into a dark, secret world, fathoms deep, where all thought was suspended, there was only the delicate torment of his fingers and lips and hands...

'Hetti... you make me lose my reason... I don't want to take you *here*—like this—in another man's bed...' His words were breathed raggedly against her hair, but she shook her head feverishly, sliding her hands along his back, tracing her nails along the ridges of muscles along his spine, outlining the rock-like jut of his pelvic bone, and feeling the hard muscles beneath the silken skin clench beneath her questing fingers with a mingled sense of disbelief and joy at the rightness, the pure joyful rightness of the feel of them together.

Now there was no turning back, a distant part of her mind was registering numbly, and it was all right... it felt right... it felt so *right*; it hadn't taken *courage* after all, just the right man, the right amount of trust... no question of second thoughts as he dragged her beneath him with a flare of wild, savage hunger, and began to thrust inside her with a hoarse groan of fulfilment, but then her involuntary gasp, the shocked clench of her muscles, brought the whole wild abandon to a shuddering halt, his breathing torn from him in huge, fierce gulps as he sought to contain and control himself, to cool the flames, sweat beading his forehead in his desperation while he searched her white face for an explanation.

'Hetti...?' He rested his damp forehead on hers, dragging long, steadying breaths, his voice rough. 'Oh, lord...Hetti...Hetti...!'

'Why did you stop?' she whispered huskily, running her fingers hungrily down his flanks, feeling another deep scar on his hip-bone and caressing it with a surging need to possess, to be possessed by him.

'Why did I stop?' He took his weight on his elbows and with ruthless self-denial he lifted himself away from her trembling body, his expression dazed. 'Hetti...in the name of *heaven*, how can you still be—why didn't you tell me this was the first time——?' He stopped abruptly, shaking his head slightly, his eyes a dark, unfathomable ocean-green as he sought to make sense of it. 'Henrietta, how *can* you be...?'

'Pure and virginal?' she whispered unsteadily, glaring frustratedly up at him through tears which were beginning to well and trickle unheeded down her temples. 'It's a long, sordid story, Nick—surely you don't want to hear it right this moment?'

He stared down at her for a long time, then he moved to one side, and taking her wet face between both hands he twisted her to face him.

'My darling girl——' He stopped, his voice thickened and choked with emotion, and with a low cry she pressed herself up against him, the violent desire he'd awoken inside her suffusing her with an impatient heat for some unknown, elusive fulfilment.

He tensed, taking her into his arms but stroking his hands over her trembling body with a kind of soothing, rhythmical action which conveyed nothing of his previous ungovernable hunger. He reached down to pull the duvet up over them, and cradled her like a child, the embrace totally undemanding. Writhing against him had no effect, and gradually, unwillingly, she let herself relax against him.

After a long while, he propped himself on his elbow, and searched her face with a kind of bewildered wonder. 'You're still a virgin—you're twenty-three years old, you've been married, you've lived with another man...and you're still a *virgin*? Would you care to tell me just what the *hell* is going on, Hetti?'

As the reckless heat began to cool she felt a wave of shame wash over her at her abandon. A coldness closed around her heart. Nick was behaving as if this made some insurmountable difference...the way he'd withdrawn from her, the way he was looking at her now... The frightening scenarios with Tristan flooded back, turning her stomach over in terror, and she sat up abruptly, uncaring of her nakedness, staring at him with a level, burning stare.

'Until now I thought I was——' she swallowed on a suddenly dry throat '—I...I thought I was frigid, Nick...'

'Frigid?' The smouldering look in his eyes made her heart start thumping madly all over again. 'My sweet girl, you're anything but that!'

'Then it's *you*...it's you that's changed everything,' she whispered huskily.

'But what about Tristan? Hetti, you *married* him! What are you saying? You got married, and then found you were completely incompatible? If you were infatuated enough to run away and marry, frankly that's the last thing I'd have expected!'

With a stifled groan of misery, she turned away. 'Oh, Nick, I don't want to... I *can't* talk about it...'

Nick reached to turn her back to him, and she saw his implacable expression as he drew her possessively into his arms. His silence held an intractable quality, an intensity that told her there was no chance any longer of hedging around those long-buried horrors.

'Tell me about it, Hetti. Please?' His fingers moved soothingly in her hair, and the soft compulsion in his voice suppressed the wave of panic.

'There *was* physical attraction between Tristan and me... I mean, of course I found him attractive... but... but he didn't seem to want an ordinary relationship.'

'Go on.'

'Oh, lord, I find this so hard to talk about... I... I suppose I shouldn't have been so *prim* and prudish...' She took a deep, shuddering breath. 'The result of having a vicar for a father, Tristan always said! You see I didn't want to... to sleep with Tristan until we got married. So it wasn't until *after* we got married that I found out he preferred *sharing* his women—unless it was somehow perverted, he simply couldn't... couldn't become...'

'... aroused?' Nick suggested gently, the gentleness of his voice a total contrast to the searing anger in his eyes. 'And he couldn't understand why you turned off completely whenever he suggested an audience?'

'Oh, Nick... it was so... *degrading*! Everything I'd ever felt for Tristan just... just vanished the moment I realised what he was really like, underneath the façade...'

'Was that when he started hitting you?'

'Maybe; he used to drink a lot after we...after it...after it all went wrong...'

She realised that she'd pulled the sheet up to cover herself, unknowingly, and she couldn't bring herself to meet Nick's eyes. She felt rigid with tension, and she sensed, rather than felt, a similar tension in him. Revulsion, she told herself achingly—he doesn't want me any more...

'Does it...does it change everything?' she whispered, agonised suddenly in the terror of losing him.

'Change everything?' he echoed harshly, his deep voice incredulous. Gently, firmly, he took her hands in his, letting the clutched sheet slip back down to her waist, and putting a finger beneath her chin he turned her white face up to his. 'Hetti, do you imagine finding out you were...*tormented* like that—hell, I don't know, *abused*— by a drunken lout I'd have personally thrown into the Thames if he hadn't already fallen in by himself...do you imagine that changes my feelings for you?'

She read the blaze of emotion in his eyes, and swallowed back her tears. 'Maybe not...but, please, Nick, don't hate Tristan,' she whispered.

He drew her close against him, crushing her hard to the deep thud of his heart, and she shivered and wrapped her arms thankfully around him.

'I felt so guilty. Maybe if I'd been more mature, I could have brought him round, shown him how I wanted our relationship to be...but he made me feel so...so *disgusted*, I just froze whenever he came near me!'

'You have no need to feel guilty. Let it go, Hetti. It's in the past, and it may be extremely selfish of me but I find I'm thanking the gods Tristan only beat you up, and stopped short of forcing you to participate in his little perversions!'

It was a long time before either of them spoke again.

'Poor Tristan,' she said at last, her voice muffled against the hard warmth of Nick's chest, 'I did love him in a way, Nick, but I just couldn't...I couldn't let myself do what he wanted...'

The tears were threatening again, and Nick pushed her slightly away, gave her a gentle shake.

'Don't, Hetti...that's the past, remember? *Now* is here, with me...though lord knows I don't deserve you. I've spent the major part of my life so far ducking personal commitments, running like hell from showing my real feelings...' His voice thickened slightly. 'So I'm having a job believing I'm the lucky man you've saved yourself for, my darling...'

She lifted her lips for his kiss, and the following few minutes were lost in a mounting heat which Nick had to determinedly douse, putting her from him with a wry twist of his mouth.

'I still don't understand where Martin fits in?' he queried softly, his lidded eyes roaming hungrily over her body.

'I *told* you about Martin. He's just a friend—more my friend than Tristan's friend, even though he was best man, as well as being the brother of my oldest school-friend—that's why I knew I could trust him when I had to get away from Tris. He's abroad on a course, at the moment—that's why I've got the use of his room...' She dashed her hand over her eyes to dry her tears, her throat tight. 'Nick, I wanted to give myself to you just now...and you've turned the tables on me. Does my virginity make such a difference? Don't you want me any more, now you know the truth?'

With a muffled curse, he pulled her back into his arms. 'My darling Henrietta...' His voice was so gentle, it made her want to cry all over again, and he tightened his arms round her. 'If you're in any doubt about how much I want you, feel me...' He took her hand and drew it down to the rigid heat of his loins, with a low, husky laugh as she stiffened against him. 'Do you feel? Are you convinced my body wants your body? Here, now, in private, with absolutely no perversions whatsoever?'

'Yes...' Heat was creeping up her neck, and she hid her face against the coarse hardness of his chest. 'But it's different for you. You do this kind of thing all the time...'

He expelled his breath on a long, shuddering out-breath, and gave her a slight shake. 'Not this kind of thing... This is a first for me, too, Henrietta...'

'You mean not taking the goods when they're on free offer?'

'Will you stop sniping?' he chided gently, his expression so tender she blinked, half dazed by the emotions he could arouse in her. 'I may not have led an entirely celibate life, but since you walked into my office for an interview three months ago, my sex life has been entirely *cerebral*...'

'Sounds vaguely disgusting. Does that mean you weren't sleeping with Joelle?' Her laugh was unsteady.

'I've never slept with Joelle. Interfering in other people's marriages is not my style, despite what the gossips might say and despite any ideas Joelle might have on the subject. Oh, hell, what am I saying? All I've done is think and dream about making love to one person...'

'Me?' She breathed it shakily.

'You...and so help me, right now I'm having the devil's own job keeping my hands off you.'

'Then why...?'

'Because there's far more to my feelings for you than a physical hunger.' He stopped, his tone filled with such intensity she shivered slightly. 'And I'm damned if I'll take advantage of your incredible...inexperience...here, now, in someone else's bed, with you, heaven help me, recovering from the flu.'

'How can you be so...so *prosaic*?' she protested weakly, struggling to free herself sufficiently to look into his face, her heart contracting joyously at the blaze of emotion in his eyes. 'Can't you see how *humiliating* this is for me? I've finally plucked up the courage to offer my meagre charms to a man, and he turns me down?'

'You think I'm being prosaic? Would it help if I said you captured my heart, that first day you walked back into my life? That I've sinced acknowledged the dubious truth that I've wanted you, to varying degrees, ever since you so enchantingly lost your jeans when I pulled your dog out of that bloody mill-sluice, that day on the cliffs?'

'But...that was nine years ago! You're not saying you actually *fancied* me, flat-chested, in pigtails and brace?' Her heart was thumping wildly, her small, fragile bud of happiness gradually expanding until it felt as if her heart were full of spring flowers.

'I did. And it may be nine years ago but I can recall you definitely were not flat-chested...' His gaze roamed down over the proud, high jut of her breasts, kindling with such heat she felt her stomach melting all over again.

'I'd have been two years under-age,' she teased softly.

'I'm well aware of that.' The deep voice was grimly ironic.

'And what about Annette?'

'Annette...' For a second, she thought he wasn't going to answer, then he smiled at her, dispelling the fear. 'Annette? She was... *my* first great infatuation. Maybe we all need one? She taught me a lesson, I suppose. It's taken me quite a while to break free from that lesson. I thought she was all mine, you see. And then she decided that Bevan had a much more lucrative future in the family business and set her sights on him. After Bevan died, she took quite a time trying to convince me I'd been her first choice all along...'

'So what happened to her in the end?'

'She married an amazingly rich sheep-farmer and went to live in New Zealand...' He stopped, twisting round to look steadily into her face, the expression in his heavy-lidded gaze making her heart leap. 'Annette is history. Forget her...'

'Gillian had a theory that you took up flying to forget Annette...'

'Did she, indeed? I went up in my first light aircraft when I was sixteen, so somewhere along the line Gillian has got her facts mixed up...'

'Mmmm...' Despite their intimacy, despite this new, scarcely believable vibration of warmth and love between them, she felt her heart in her mouth as she summoned courage to ask the next question. 'That dinner I had with Marc, he...he had a theory that you avoid commitment to any one woman because life—in the shape of Annette—has taught you to be cautious...and...and *Joelle* said you preferred more mature, married women like her, because you were terrified of getting *trapped* in a relationship... Is that true, Nick?'

There was a brief silence, and she almost held her breath.

'If those theories are correct,' Nick said slowly, patiently, his gaze steady, 'how come for the last three months I've thought of nothing but finding some way to finish up with you standing beside me in your father's church in St Wenna, saying "Forsaking all other, keep thee only unto her, so long as ye both shall live"?'

She blinked, stunned. 'Truly? You want to marry me? When all the time you've treated me as if you loathed and despised me?'

He groaned softly. 'Oh, hell, of course I want to marry you, my darling! I know I've been foul—can you forgive me? I've been so flayed with jealousy at the thought of any other man, past, present or future, taking the place I longed to be in!'

'Oh, Nick...'

'This last couple of weeks have been the worst weeks of my life. Every morning, when I woke up, I knew I had to come and find you... and by the evening I'd convinced myself to stay out of your way, because you detested me...'

'I never detested you! I realised, that night when I'd had dinner with Marc, that I love you... No, I think I must have known before that, I just wouldn't let myself admit it...'

His fingers wound themselves in her hair, threading possessively through the blonde and brown, his gaze intent. 'When I played the violin and you sang with me,' he said softly, 'that was the first ray of hope. The look in your eyes afterwards nearly drove me mad...I've been

in torment ever since…and if you knew how I've longed
to hear you say you love me, you wouldn't have flung
those three precious words so casually into that last sentence of yours!'

She gave him a dazzling smile, putting her hand against
his cheek and stroking his face wonderingly. 'Don't look
at me like that…not if you're refusing to do anything
about it—it's not fair on my blood-pressure… What
have you been doing since I left Cornwall?' she breathed
shakily.

'I had to go to France for a couple of days, sort things
out over there…I bought that old manor by the river
at Pont-Ménel, then wished I hadn't because I knew I
wanted to share it with you, and you hated me…I don't
think I've been *numèro uno* in popularity at the office,
either.' He grinned ruefully. 'In fact I harassed the life
out of an abysmal temp, until Gillian took pity on me
and came back. Then when I'd cooled down over Piers,
I realised I'd have to go and sort things out with
him…and then when he told me where you'd gone to
live, all my noble intentions of leaving you in peace vanished overnight…'

'I'm glad they did…' The husky tremble in her voice
made his arms tighten cruelly hard around her, and she
swallowed back the ridiculous tears. 'I'm sorry.' She
sniffed helplessly, burying her face against his shoulder
again. 'I keep wanting to cry…'

'It's the after-effects of the flu,' Nick said softly, and
she turned her face up to see him smiling down at her
with such heart-stopping tenderness she had to bite her
lip to control her surge of emotion.

'No, it's not. You've cured my flu. It's the way I feel...sort of torn apart with happiness. Is that possible, do you think?'

'Highly possible, if the way I'm feeling is anything to go by...' He gave her a gentle shake, and risked a gentle kiss on her lips. 'You seem to have been very busy discussing me, incidentally...there I was believing you hadn't the slightest interest in me. What other riveting little snippets of gossip have you been listening to?'

'Helen told me you had a fearful reputation with women...and Marc said the reason you always insist on driving, even in other people's cars, is because of the accident with Bevan... Is that true?'

She felt him tense a fraction in her arms, then relax again. 'The reputation—well, we could all do with a little less gossip surrounding us at times, don't you agree?'

'Amen to that.'

'The driving thing...Marc's probably right there. Do you mind marrying a paranoid?'

'I expect I'll adjust. As long as you give me free flying lessons!'

'It's a deal...Hetti, about Piers——'

'No, don't let's talk about Piers.'

'We have to. I'm sorry about the things I said that morning. I blew my top—it was as much jealousy over your night out with Marc as anything your brother had inflicted on me!'

'But you'd spent the night with Joelle!'

'Like hell I had! I cut the tour short, came back to see you about Piers, and discovered Marc had left Joelle a message at their hotel saying he'd taken you out for dinner.'

'Well, it was *only* dinner...'

'Yes, I know...' Nick's voice was softly ragged against her hair, and she shivered and slid her arms round him.

'I was so jealous, thinking of you spending the night with Joelle. It hurt, like . . . like toothache!'

He gave a low laugh, and kissed her neck. 'I had no intention of staying overnight somewhere with Joelle, even if the Piers crisis hadn't blown up in my face!'

She was silent, absorbing this reassurance with a glow of happiness. Eventually she murmured, 'Thank you for giving Piers another chance. He doesn't deserve it.'

'Piers will behave himself from now on.' Nick's tone held an underlying note of steel. 'And he has the makings of a very good estate agent—if I didn't believe that, I wouldn't have taken him back . . .'

'But would you have taken him back if he weren't my brother?' she probed softly.

Nick expelled his breath slowly. 'Probably not. But the brother of the woman I love has to win some perks, don't you think?'

There was a lengthy silence. The heat was building up between them again, and her blood seemed to be singing wildly through her veins at the feel of his hard body so close to hers.

'I think we'd better get some clothes back on,' Nick said nobly, his voice slightly thicker, huskier, as if reading her mind. 'Otherwise this current set of good intentions is going to vanish like all the others, and your friend might just come back to find us in a compromising situation.'

'Clare won't be back until much later . . .'

'Don't tempt me, siren . . .' He reached to retrieve her nightdress from its far-flung heap on the floor, but when he handed it to her with a wry grin she made no move to put it on, pushing back the bed-covers and kneeling up on the bed, her gaze steady and wide-eyed, facing him unselfconsciously, as if being naked in bed with Nick Trevelyan was suddenly the most natural thing in the world.

'I love you, Nick,' she said simply.

A tinge of deeper colour crept along his high cheek-bones as he returned her stare. 'And I love you. You *will* marry me? Quickly?'

Her smile was luminous as she reached out to offer both her hands into the warmth of his. 'If that's what it takes to remedy my horribly old-fashioned virginity,' she whispered shakily, 'I suppose I'll have to!'

Four weeks later she was sitting at a breakfast table in a sunny bay window overlooking the river, spreading butter with unabashed hedonism on a croissant still warm from the *boulangerie* in the village, and reading parts of a letter out loud between ecstatic mouthfuls.

'Can you believe my family?' She shot a wide-eyed, laughing glance at Nick. 'Writing to me on my *honey-moon* and wondering if I'm pregnant yet?'

Nick gazed at her blandly, his expression hard to fathom. 'I always knew I liked your family. Send them a postcard saying I'm doing my best.'

'I suppose they're direct and to the point,' she agreed drily, ignoring his teasing grin, scanning the pages for any more gems. 'My mother has rediscovered how much she likes *your* mother after meeting her again at the wedding.' She shot a dancing glance at Nick and saw his grimace with a bubble of laughter welling up inside her. 'And . . . good heavens, Piers has split up from Amy and he's seeing *Clare*! That should be much better for him—if Clare can't knock Piers into shape, no one can...'

Nick stood up, and came round the table to inspect the letter laughingly over her shoulder. 'Fascinating...' he assured her evenly, sliding his hands down over her shoulders and beginning to part the pale aqua satin lapels of her wrap, so that she caught her breath jerkily. 'But, much as I adore your family, and tolerate my dear mother, let's not forget they're part of the reason why we're hiding over here in the peace of the French countryside!'

'Mmmm... We'll have to go back and face them all again at some point...'

'True, but we've always got this place to retreat to when the going gets tough!'

She gave a gurgle of laughter and caught his hand in hers, her heart brimming over with love and happiness. 'It's so beautiful here...like another world...' she murmured, picking up her coffee-cup and gazing through the deep window embrasure in a commendable effort to dispel the growing shivers of desire from Nick's seeking fingers. The thickly wooded river wound peacefully past the manor house, and their ketch bobbed gently, sails furled, just visible at its mooring on the private jetty. 'I still can't believe you bought it so *quickly*—in England you'd still be waiting for surveys or searches or being gazumped or something.'

Nick grinned, the crinkle of genuine amusement around his eyes never failing to set her pulses racing hectically, to remind her of the indescribable happiness she'd found at last. 'The French system is different. You should know that, as my newly appointed director in charge of French sales!'

'*Vive la différence?*'

'Agreed, as long as the old place doesn't come crashing down around our ears due to the lack of time-consuming surveys!'

'Pessimist.'

Their eyes met and held, and she put her coffee-cup down with a slightly unsteady hand, responding to the narrowed gleam in Nick's green eyes with a tinge of heat in her cheeks. 'Nick, we've only just got up...'

'I'm only hoping to oblige my new mother-in-law...and, besides, can I help it if the sight of my new bride having breakfast in that revealing little scrap of satin makes my thoughts turn inevitably back to bed?' he queried plaintively, holding out his hand to her with a laughing appraisal. 'Are you actually wearing anything at all under there, Mrs Trevelyan?'

'Not a stitch, Mr Trevelyan...and if I'd known you were such a lecher I'd never have married you...'

'I thought that was precisely why you did marry me. So don't preach to me about my *debauched* appetites, and give me a sneak preview, my love...'

Twisting around to him, she linked her arms round his neck and lifted her parted lips to his with a soft, impatient groan of desire, and he lifted her in his arms and carried her up to the large shadowy bedroom, decorated in shades of green and white and gold to reflect the colours of the garden and the river beyond, and placed her almost reverently in the centre of the wide, white-covered bed.

'Love me...love me now...' It was a shuddering sigh before they melted together in the immense, miraculous emotion which enveloped them whenever mouths and bodies came in contact, still a source of confusion and bewildered joy to Henrietta even in the third week of her honeymoon.

'Oh, Nick...' She laughed huskily up at him, as he dispensed with his own black cords and sweatshirt and then bent to slide the satin robe slowly, inch by silken inch, from her body, kissing each exposed part of her in turn until she was writhing urgently, needing no further arousal, the trembling heat inside her more than enough to demand fulfilment.

'Stop teasing,' she whispered achingly, catching her fingers rapturously in his thick dark hair and pulling him impatiently down to her. 'You know I hate being teased.'

'And you know how I love teasing you, my wanton little wife...'

With a blaze of heat in his eyes, he bent his head and let his tongue trace the parted outline of her mouth, then slid it between her lips in shuddering simulation of the sexual act as he thrust her fiercely beneath him and finally, victoriously, took possession of her.

'Now, Hetti?' he murmured huskily, his lidded gaze like molten emerald on her face, as he began to move, slowly at first, then with gathering rhythm.

'Oh, yes...yes!' The time for teasing was past. The force unleashed between them was too great, the mounting path to that astonishing, feverish peak of pleasure too inevitable. When she felt the power of his climax, her fingers dug convulsively into his back, as the rigid clench of her muscles, with the glorious eruption of shock waves radiating from that one taut, piercing moment, spun her out into another world, another space, and she cried out his name, raggedly, and then lay, spent and shivering, in the possessive circle of his arms.

'Oh, Nick...' When she could speak again, it felt as if someone had filled her veins with champagne. 'If you knew how you make me feel when you make love to me like that...'

'Powerful?' he hazarded softly, his eyes dark with love as they roamed down over the contours of her body.

'Feminine...supremely female...Nick, I'm so happy! I never knew it was possible to be this happy! I'm so gloriously, incredibly happy, being married to you!'

A slight shudder ran through him, and his arms tightened around her, his fingers raking through her hair, then sliding provocatively along the sensitive nape of her neck.

'The feeling, Mrs Trevelyan, is mutual.' His husky assurance, the stroking of his hands, told her that even now his need for her was far from sated.

'So you do still love me?' she teased softly, stroking her hands slowly over the strong, harsh angles of his body.

'I love you more every day—haven't you been listening to a word I've said these past four weeks?'

'Well, maybe just occasionally...'

'You're mine, Hetti—nobody else's. I'll always love you...'

'And I'll always love you...' It was a low, fierce whisper as she turned her head against his chest, feeling the strength of his arms with a sigh of pure contentment. 'I'm yours—nobody else's—your very own private property, Nick Trevelyan...'

'And I'm busy putting up "No Trespassing" signs, my darling...and heaven help anyone who tries to get past them...'

His laughing voice held a ragged note of tenderness which dispelled even the last, most stubborn of her secret fears, and Henrietta wriggled happily into his arms, closed her eyes, and let the rapture and the wonder begin all over again, secure in the dawning, glorious knowledge that no matter what had happened in the past, right here and now she was exactly where she had always belonged...

Mills & Boon

Next month's Romances

Each month, you can choose from a world of variety in romance with Mills & Boon. These are the new titles to look out for next month.

UNLIKELY CUPID Catherine George

HEART ON FIRE Charlotte Lamb

BLIND PASSION Anne Mather

WITHOUT KNOWING WHY Jessica Steele

A LITTLE MOONLIGHT Betty Neels

NO WAY TO BEGIN Michelle Reid

ANYTHING FOR YOU Rosemary Hammond

MAGIC CARPETS Lucy Keane

PIRATE'S HOSTAGE Eleanor Rees

A FOOLISH DREAM Emma Richmond

ONCE IN A LIFETIME Jacqueline Gilbert

THE RELUCTANT LOVER Miranda Lee

THE IMPERFECT BRIDE Karen van der Zee

FORGOTTEN LOVE Nicola West

TENDER BETRAYAL Grace Green

STARSIGN
A DESIRE TO LOVE Sally Cook

Available from Boots, Martins, John Menzies, W.H. Smith, Woolworths and other paperback stockists.

Also available from Mills and Boon Reader Service, P.O. Box 236, Thornton Road, Croydon, Surrey CR9 3RU.

Three women, three loves . . . Haunted by one dark, forbidden secret.

Margaret – a corner of her heart would always remain Karl's, but now she had to reveal the secrets of their passion which still had the power to haunt and disturb.

Miriam – the child of that forbidden love, hurt by her mother's little love for her, had been seduced by Israel's magic and the love of a special man.

Hannah – blonde and delicate, was the child of that love and in her blue eyes, Margaret could again see Karl.

It was for the girl's sake that the truth had to be told, for only by confessing the secrets of the past could Margaret give Hannah hope for the future.

W●RLDWIDE

Accept 4 Free Romances and 2 Free gifts

• FROM MILLS & BOON •

An irresistible invitation from Mills & Boon Reader Service. Please accept our offer of 4 free romances, a CUDDLY TEDDY and a special MYSTERY GIFT... Then, if you choose, go on to enjoy 6 more exciting Romances every month for just £1.45 each postage and packing free. Plus our FREE newsletter with author news, competitions and much more.

Send the coupon below at once to: Reader Service, FREEPOST, P.O. Box 236, Croydon, Surrey CR9 9EL

✂ — — — — — — NO STAMP NEEDED — — — — —

YES! Please rush me my 4 Free Romances and 2 FREE Gifts! Please also reserve me a Reader Service Subscription so I can look forward to receiving 6 Brand New Romances each month for just £8.70, post and packing free. If I choose not to subscribe I shall write to you within 10 days. I understand I can keep the free books and gifts whatever I decide. I can cancel or suspend my subscription at any time. I am over 18 years of age.

Name Mr/Mrs/Miss _____ EP86R

Address _____

_____

_____ Postcode _____

Signature _____